THE TEMPLAR
AND THE CROSS OF CHRIST

Part Three

Nigel Clayton

The National Library of Australia Cataloguing-in-Publication
data:

Vassal, Pierre. [pseudonym]
ISBN 978 0 6489 863 3 1
I. Title.
A823.4

BISAC
DRA018000 Drama / Medieval
FIC009100 Fiction / Fantasy / Action & Adventure
FIC026000 Fiction / Religious

Epic poems by this author:

Kibeho: An Epic Poem
Afghan - Song of the Desert
Orcinus Orca - Song of the Ocean
Hollandia Nova, 1712 - Song of the Coast
Song of the Templar

Other titles by this author:

Dreamtime - An Aboriginal Odyssey
Templar, Assassination, Trial & Torture
Underworld
The Long Road to Rwanda
The Templar: and the City of God [Part 1]
The Templar: and the Temple of Káros [Part 2]

You should not give in to evils,
but proceed ever more boldly against them.

 *One*

Abu, The Strangler, sat back, his feet upon the small desk of his cramped cabin. The news on the enemy was good. He felt as relaxed as he could ever feel, totally in command of his senses and his destiny.

Abu rarely conferred with others, seeking not their opinion on matters of military importance, but in this particular case it was decided that, to allow voices to be heard, would strengthen the weakened morale of all on board. So weak they were, so weak that Abu could not see how they could call themselves men, lacking in pride and spirit. He cast himself so high above those around him that he felt as though he had only one thing in common with them, and that was his religion.

So they had gathered, Abu, Ibrahim, Ahmad, Sherif and Mollet; Abu the commander, Ibrahim for he was a lamb which was easily swayed, Abu for familiarity, Ahmad for his official rank, Sherif for his ability to bully opinions to his favour, and Mollet to influence the rowers, to enforce courage and to free them of their tormented defeat against the Christians. Abu pounded the small desk then, infuriated at the embarrassment that he had been forced to endure. The very thought that the Christians had escaped his net was almost too much to handle; but the current situation did lend a little optimism.

It would seem that all aboard the Christian carrack were completely unaware as to the mahon that followed; but that was absurd. Abu shook the thought from his head and then considered it again. How could the weeks, which were gathering in number and falling behind them, not bear some form of

5

caution to which the Christians could use to their advantage? It was clear that the crow's nest of the Christian boat was manned, both day and night, for a lantern could be clearly seen high above the crest of the waves which formed between the two boats; they, therefore, could see them as well as they could see the Christians.

The verdict was simple; the Christians knew what followed in their wake but cared little, so long as the mahon maintained its distance. So what would the Christians do if the mahon made a move to attack? Make for shore? Seek the protection of a nearby coastal city? As for the reason behind their current situation whereby the Christians were avoiding quite purposely any contact with another vessel of European cast, there was only one reason which came to mind: the chest of secrets.

The chest of secrets; it was Abu's new curse. He had to have the chest, at any cost: his men, his high position and rank, his recognition of professionalism; it all mattered little to him now, for he was to gain upon a new destiny, new riches, a rewarding life.

Abu stood and announced to all the orders which he had contemplated over their time following the carrack. "We shall deliver our clothes to the hungry sea and take to masquerade. We must sail towards the coast and attack the first vessel we see. We shall dress as the European dresses and seek out the carrack once more, aboard another boat, to avert scrutiny. We shall be seen to be nothing more than another boatload of Christians." And one final plea was needed to ensure they maintained their obscurity. "We must pray no more whilst in public, we must learn to do without our praise to God whilst before a Christian, for we must teach ourselves to be as a Christian; after all, how else will we be able to get closer to the chest and its grand reward?"

And so, with orders so struck the mahon did attack a Christian boat within three days, and within another three weeks they caught glimpse of the enemy carrack once more as it made its way towards safe harbour. The carrack was approaching the coast and had an hour's advantage on the, now, Muslim's brigantine. But Abu had considered much over the past few months and it seemed to him that the orphans upon the vessel to their front would affect the ability of the Christian men to make any reasonable time in escape once on land. Abu had also considered the possibility that those aboard the carrack would alert the authorities upon the shore of the enemies, their approach, even if they did appear European.

Abu looked over to the horizon and saw an opportunity. Fast approaching was a storm, and it seemed to be large and ferocious, for lightning could be seen and heard as it struck out with its tentacles of destruction. He would use it to his advantage; take what he could from what was offered. He may have to make for land some distance from any port that fell before them, even go so far as abandoning ship; but he could also press his luck and stay upon the heel of his adversary.

Time would tell; but time was also short.

Two

Tu ne cede malis, sed contra audentior ito

In times of war the landscape changes much, as do the borders of countries, lands conquered and then won back. What is France one day is not necessarily the same on another; what is Spain at one time is also of the same equation. This was the result of war, where constant conflict between countries affected the religion of people and their loyalties. Most of the humble of any country were the poor, and the poor wanted nothing more than to be left alone, to plant and harvest their crops, to be able to feed their families and live in peace. But man does not always get what he wants; quite seldom in actual fact would a peasant be content with his life and status but peace was always hungered for.

From Stephen and with his insight of the Lord came knowledge of the safe haven which they did seek; none other than Barcelona. It was a reasonably small town which relied heavily upon the fishing industry. It was the voice which had been delivered to him, another to join the many he had received, but the voices themselves did slow to a trickle, until some three weeks before entering port the voices ceased to occur altogether. Stephen felt as though blinded by sight for he had relied on them for answers, and for comfort. But the dreams had steered him well. Not a night would go by without his slumber being intruded by a dream of some description. Sure enough, he dreamt like any other man, but he also had dreams which could only be considered as godly, for the voices of the day had become his dreams of night, where messages would be passed onto him from the heavens above.

The evening was cold and wet, a little drizzle falling upon the earth and sea, clouds commencing to thicken more than they were before, blackening upon the horizon and drifting ever closer, the dark mass of terror approaching fast. The ferocity of the storm was of little concern to Stephen and the others for they were so close to stepping on dry land that cover could readily be sought from the evil about to be lashed out upon the coast.

It was a slow approach towards harbour, all aboard taking in the surroundings, endeavouring to learn a little, even if non-productive, in order to prepare themselves for when they departed the safety of their carrack. It was not at all busy, for the fishing boats of the area had already dispersed with their catch of the day. It was clear to all that no boat or ship would be getting ready for the sea due to the approaching storm, which would be upon them at any minute, the little, light rain falling upon the deck soon gathering more body and thus a weightier fall from the sky above.

They moored themselves at a vacant slot upon the pier, the only vacant spot to be seen in the harbour; most boats and ships had taken the warning from what could be seen and had secured themselves as best they could.

Quite suddenly a fat-bellied man with red cheeks and small ledger in hand came running up, pushing his way through a small gathering, between groups of men in their twos and threes. He was seemingly agitated by the approach and mooring of the carrack, as his soon to be voiced displeasure was to reveal.

"Who is it, I command, that sees fit to tie fast upon this pier?" yelled the harbour master, slowing his run to a walk, a quickened stride delivering him to where the carrack came to an unsteady halt. He was somewhat out of breath and took in a few quick mouthfuls of air, satisfying his urgent need for oxygen.

"Stephen is my name." Stephen stood tall and stepped upon the wooden decking where he was being moored. Stephen looked temporarily around to the others at work, seeing that all had conveyed to his request by having removed their Order's regalia. Now they resembled nothing more than sailors fit for the sea, with swords hanging from their belts, swords, mind you, not common amongst men of the sea who did nothing more than fish for a living.

"Stephen, ah; well tell me, by what manner have you secured the permission to strap fast to this here pier?" said the harbour master, his eyes squinting, looking upon Stephen as though to scold him, the fresh breeze blowing at his thick head of hair. A sudden shiver then came over him, his shoulders shaking, as though shook by the hand of God.

"None," said Stephen, shrugging his shoulders through defiant disregard for the harbour master's concerns, which was delivered with such simplicity that the fat-bellied oxen stammered.

"None, indeed. Well, to moor here will cost you plenty, and up-front if you please," said the harbour master, anxious to find some coin in his fist. It was his way and his pleasure, to tax those that dared to trespass upon his ground.

"Dear sir, as you can see, we are nothing more than poor wretches whose only cargo it that of children," the fat-bellied harbour master looked beyond Stephen and could see the children gathered next to the rail of the carrack, "and a few men of the sea, sailors all, as good as any other; as you can clearly see. Now if you look yonder," and to this, Stephen looked into the distance, "you will see our escort." Stephen gave further indication to the Muslim craft with pointed finger, still some distance off from shore.

"A brigantine," said the harbour master, undecided on the boat's character or importance, it being too far out for him to make a solid opinion. But if it was true, and it was indeed an escort ship, he could be well fitted with compensation.

"Yes sir. Our Lord and master sails in our wake, protection granted us on this, our long, long voyage, for he dislikes children," said Stephen, reflecting a little on the harbour master, pondering on what he was thinking.

"And from where do you come, weighted down with so few men and a score of children?"

"Orphans, one and all," replied Stephen

"Orphans, maybe, but that does not answer my question. And of the sailors that you command; from where do you all come?"

"Please respect us. My master will pay all you need, but for now I must get these children to shore. As you can clearly see, poor weather is approaching fast. The children's needs must be taken into immediate consideration." And to make his quest as real as could be he asked of the harbour master, "And where is your nearest convent?"

"To be found up the road, towards the east," answered the fat man. "It is quite easy to find and has a cross chiselled within the stone above the door.

"Thank you, kind sir." Stephen turned then to all those on board, their eyes glued to him now, for their work was done; the men had completed their tasks and the children had congregated upon the deck. "Gather you things, children, though little I know your possessions to be, for we set out for the convent as promised."

Some of the children looked to one another, lost as to what Stephen had just commanded in regards to 'my master', but others who had listened closely to what the knight had said before entering the harbour quietly offered advice, 'do as you are told', 'pretend to adhere to orders,' and 'Stephen is stalling, quickly gather your things, nuns will aid us,' for the brigantine following could only be of a single nationality and Stephen knew which. They had no time to lose and needed to gain as much distance from the pier, or to find safe haven, as quickly as possible. The things that were gathered were little to say the least, and of weapons, the children left those behind, for the last thing they needed was to draw attention upon themselves.

"But what of my pay?" asked the fat man, drawing upon the fact that his palm was still empty and his appetite for greed had not yet been quenched.

"My master shall pay when he sets to shore, but until then, if it helps to settle you, you may keep our carrack until payment has been received by the silk of your purse. Ours is not to deceive and our master will pay, but we must attend to the children's needs."

To the man it seemed a fair agreement, as fair as any other, under the circumstance. Good condition the boat was thought, and considered, to be in, but unbeknown to any one around the boat had a weak spot in the hull, which could be easily breached under stressing circumstance.

With that the man smiled and all aboard the carrack commenced to unload themselves, along with the chest of secrets, a chest so beautifully designed and mystifying that the harbour master had to give it a second look. "What is in the chest? Gold?"

"No gold," said Stephen, "just private possession that the convent will require once we have unloaded the burden of these children upon them."

"Uh, ah. And the carrack?" he asked. "A good boat is she?"

"The best, for she bought us most of the way from Constantinople."

"Constantinople, ah; please, what is the news?" The harbour master gave genuine interest, for news of Constantinople came little these days. All he knew was of the siege lasting for what seemed to be forever. It was the talk of any town along the coast of the Mediterranean.

"She, the city so grand, is now in Muslim hands." And with that the harbour master stood shocked and watched, as the crew and children stepped from the boat, and they made their way towards dry land for the first time in many weeks.

"Gather children, men too, come close," said Stephen to the others, the rain now coming down quite solidly, growing in its intensity.

All gathered around, in an alley shadowed by buildings either side, passers-by looking upon them briefly as they continued upon their business. It was good that the storm provided them with so much cover from curiosity and that few people, rushing to get away from the approaching storm, had little time to ponder the loitering of seven men and thirteen children.

"We continue as planned, no stragglers, no idle chatter. We must attend our mission with purpose; remember your tasks and complete them well. I shall see you all soon." The knights nodded in acceptance of their tasks, tasks which had been developed to cater for their situation, tasks which would grant them their need to finally uncover the secret of the chest, to fuse the contents, to reap the reward which was to be inherited by them all.

"We shall miss you, Stephen," said Catherine, the other children in agreement, their voices starting to rise. Stephen in particular had a lot of love for Catherine. She had proven to be quite the fighter and at such a young age. It was clear to him from the moment the Muslims tried to board their Brigantine that Catherine was a very special child.

"Please, good children. You shall not be deserted." Stephen held Catherine momentarily as she came in for a hug and a little comfort, to feel the security offered by his presence. They then released each other. "I shall be back soon. You heed well to what Martin has to say, Raoul too," and he looked into the eyes of the two knights he had just named, seeing them smile in return as they passed on their silent word to take care of the children or die in the process of their protection. Each and every one of the knights had the same quality. Not only were they pure but they carried that instilled kindness and caring, a strength of character that could not be questioned.

The children fell silent and each came in to hug Stephen close, as Catherine had done before them. Stephen got down upon his knees to accept them, to return their affection and feeling. "I shall miss you all, one and the same. But we shall be together again soon; trust me," and with the word 'trust' came smiles filled with joy, for Stephen could not lie to any of them, any more than he could lie to the Lord in Heaven.

Stephen glanced at the two knights, Martin and Raoul, and smiled, a final nod being exchanged. It was time for each to go their separate ways, grouped in their pairs as Stephen had ordered; Martin with Raoul, Lars with Aaron, and Lambert and

Bernard with Stephen.

"Come, children," said Martin, "follow me now, for the nuns will take care of you until Stephen's triumphant return." The children turned and followed Martin, moving from the alley and into the fuller force of the gale that was brewing, and Raoul followed up from the rear whilst keeping an eye open for any one of them that might inadvertently fall behind. The other men looked upon Stephen as though some empowering hybrid, being of religion and military influence so grand that it could never be washed away.

"Aaron, you stay here with Lars, watch the brigantine and its crew as we discussed. You have a little time to play with, for the brigantine is still some distance away, but watch your step, all of you."

"Why, Stephen, why did you not say something to the harbour master, get him to ring the alarm?" asked Bernard.

"It is too hard to have them slaughtered, too hard to prove. I do pity them, for they know not of the devil within them, and besides, they might not be those that followed us during the first part of our journey, I am simply employing logic. The harbour master also needed to believe that he would be paid for our mooring." Stephen placed a comforting hand upon Aaron in reflection of Bernard's query. "Watch the children from a distance, and the heathen Turk most of all; remain safe, the Turks might wish to... see them. The last thing we need is for one or all of the children to fall captive."

Aaron smiled and stepped out from the shadow leaving Lars to shake hands with Stephen before he parted company. "Farewell, Lars. Partake of some refreshment if you so desire, but remain clear headed. The children must stay safe. And when I return I shall wish to know the whereabouts of the Turks. We need to understand fully their disposition in order to organise our getaway."

Lars nodded and retreated with Aaron into the growing storm as it continued to unveil itself.

"Which leaves just a few," added Stephen. "Let us find some

shelter, far from here." And with that Bernard and Lambert followed with the chest carried between them both, heading out of the alley and then along the road to the north, the handles of the chest which they carried cutting into their palms, the cold tormenting their fingers, the effort praying a little upon their minds.

Some good fortune was to be had, however, for it was in their favour that the wind and rain lashed at their backs, the strength of the wind helping to carry them up the hills that they encountered during their short trek, a trek in which they were searching for one man of singular importance. They were seeking a priest, one that resided a short distance from town, several hours or more by foot, depending on the extremes of weather that they were to be confronted by.

Three

Tu ne cede malis, sed contra audentior ito

The story of Aaron.

Aaron was nothing more than a peasant, of little interest to anyone except his mother, nothing of interest at all, in particular to a knight.

It was Sir Godfrey of Renne le Chateau, on the coast of the Mediterranean; he was straddled high upon his horse wearing his chain mail and basinet. The horse was a large white beast, a stallion from Spain, a heavy horse which commanded a heavy price. The knight had his sword sheathed, his left palm resting upon his thigh, and his right hand steered him effortlessly with reigns held loosely. Yes indeed, he and his horse were a grand affair, his horse the best of any breed, the largest horse Aaron had seen in his entire life, which for such a life had been long and hard, even though he was only 16 years old.

The knight was approaching his mother's farm with or without good reason, trespassing, which would be allowed such a large framed man at this time. Such a spectacle of a man on horse conveyed much importance and high authority and it would be best to let him pass without delay. This in itself brought much displeasure to Aaron for he was tired of being frowned upon, tired of the poor treatment that his cast were inappropriately given, but what choice did he have but to accept it.

The knight's horse walked on and the knight, whose name was currently unknown to Aaron, looked down upon the boy before bringing his horse to a stop. Aaron had been ploughing by hand a little of the field that it was his duty to attend this day. He was covered in sweat and patches of soil had stuck to his skin. His clothing fared no better and he stank of a foul odour.

His mother's farm was not large but extremely important for the wealth of the field was their only support in this miserable, contemptible life. The last thing they needed was for it to be turned upside down. As any other peasant, farmer, or undesirable, all they wished for was to be left alone, to tend their crops and chickens, to pursue their life, showering themselves in as much luxury as their wealth could afford: which was very little to none.

"Boy; who are you boy?" said the knight from high upon his horse, looking down upon Aaron with distaste in his mouth, his facial expression spelling out his thoughts on the peasant to his front as though he had spoken out loud. "Answer, for I am Sir Godfrey of Renne le Chateau. Do you know of me?"

Aaron was unsure of what to say, and whether or not he should; but he had been given permission. "No, sir, I do not; and my name is Aaron." Why should he know this stranger? If he had indeed ever come past this way before it was when neither he nor his mother were attending to the field. Was the name and title, Sir Godfrey or Renne le Chateau, of any particular significance?

The knight looked stunned for a brief moment for the boy named Aaron did not seem to shy too long from making a response, and when the response came it was strong and with much conviction. Such strength in character must be put in its place. If a peasant was allowed to muster too much confidence then knights of honour would be treated with little respect.

"Do I scare you boy? Me upon this horse, dressed in mail and passing through your farm without permission? Aye; I see it in your eyes, boy. I see that you care not for one as humble as me trespassing upon your land."

"It is not for me to like or dislike," said Aaron in reply, "for we are a peaceful family who would not dream of asking a fee from anyone passing across our land. There is no toll here, you

may pass freely. Most would be content to use the road, but...."
Aaron trailed off, having said too much.

"But what? Speak, boy, speak what you feel," insisted the knight. He remained steady upon his horse; the only muscles moving were those around his lips and upon his forehead.

"It is for the rich to make what they will of any given situation, to take what they want and to discard the rest. We are poor farmers who know no different. I have no concern for your presence upon my mother's land. You are free to pass as you so desire. It is not for me to comment or complain."

"Is that what I am, or simply represent?" asked the knight. "Am I rich beyond your wildest dreams?"

"You have a horse, a shield, and a sword," pointed out Aaron. "You have more than I ever shall."

"Ah, I see."

"But I am not afraid, as you can tell, so maybe I am stupid," said Aaron, thinking of his mother and their place in life. "If you wish to pass, then pass. I tend this field to bring us food. I can answer your questions but I must continue with my work."

"Where is your mother?" the knight saw Aaron look over his shoulder to the farm house. "Is she alone?"

"What is it you want from us?" asked Aaron with confidence. "Do you want food and water, something for your horse perhaps?"

"Company, boy. I want to touch female flesh," answered the knight as he eyed Aaron with contempt of his own, as Aaron now looked at him. "I see by the look in your eye that you understand my meaning; now get out of my way," and with hard kicking upon the frame of his horse he tried to move towards the farm house, wishing to push the horse on as fast as he could, but that first step was the hardest for Aaron had carried himself to action.

Suddenly, with the quickest of motion, Aaron swung the tool of his trade up and around his head, bringing it in hard against the horse's front legs as it pushed past him, bringing the monstrous mount down in a heap, the knight falling over the top of his horse and into the ploughed earth. It stunned Sir Godfrey for the shortest amount of time, time enough for Aaron to give warning.

"Mother! Mother!" yelled Aaron, calling out towards the small house, giving warning to his mother, for her to prepare herself by any means possible, for it was not his deplorable life that he cared, but for the life of the one that had given birth to him.

The knight got to his feet in what appeared slow motion, Aaron holding his tool across his body in a gesture of defence, but what defence can a stick of wood have against the sharpened edge of a broadsword? It was now that the first show of terror appeared on Aaron's face, but it was short lived for he dug deep and found the courage he was seeking, courage enough to carry out any necessary action, to defend his mother and her honour.

"You will now die, boy," said the knight as he drew on his sword, the gleaming metal being released of its darkened hold within its wooden sheath. The knight had two hands gripped firmly around his weapon. He seemed to command it well, even at this, the early stage of his assault upon the thin frame of Aaron. "For I am going to cut you to shreds and deal with you mother as I see fit. Her death will not be slow." The knight came upon Aaron swiftly, bringing his sword up above his head, to slash down upon the boy's skull, to split it in two. And as he commenced his action he could see the boy did not even flinch; he was steadfast, unafraid of what was to be. The sword came down and at the last moment Aaron stepped aside, the knight finishing his swing, the sword's edge cutting into the ploughed earth. Aaron lifted his foot and kicked out at the knight, his foot connecting with the knight's shoulder, forcing him down into the dirt once more. "You are heavy with armour, heavy with sword," said Aaron, "where I am quick on my feet and able to move freely." Aaron was confident in his speech, brave with his action, and above all, in command and control of his anger.

"I shall not make the same mistake twice, boy," said the knight from there upon the field, and as he got up he continued in essence, saying without further ado, "for I am an educated man, quick at thinking, fast to learn. You are a swine, yet I envy your fast action, and pity what you are about to suffer, for I shall make yours a slow death too."

Aaron could not contemplate any situation whereby this knight would have sufficient ill feeling towards him that death and rape should be the order of the day. "What are we to you, but poor farmers? Surely a knight as yourself could have any woman you desired... Ah." And Aaron understood. This knight fed on the terror he created, he fed himself with the knowledge that he could do as he pleased. He was probably a vagabond, travelling the country and doing as he pleased. This was why Aaron should have reason to know him, for he was a wanted man: or possibly still, he had returned from war and had a taste for forced pleasure.

"That's right, boy, any I desire, and my lust if for rape."

"But, Sir Godfrey, you are forgetting one thing."

"And what is that?"

"My mother," and Aaron pointed to where his mother stood. Having heard her son call she had appeared at the door of their tiny house, had seen the calamity of the situation and had arrived at an easy decision. She had made an approach towards the scene of the knight and her son, had closed the gap so that she was within range. She now stood with a crossbow in her hand, a hunting weapon used for hunting by her deceased husband, a weapon capable of penetrating the mail that the knight wore. Even now, as the knight looked on, she stepped ever closer, making for a good target in order not to miss her mark.

"My mother is a veteran shot. She will not flinch," said Aaron coolly.

The knight stood fast. "You know that if you attempt to kill me that you will both suffer greatly and be hanged, by the noose of the rope I carry, and if you should let me go then I shall return. You cannot win."

"We are not afraid, sir knight," said Aaron with further contempt that fury built up within the knight to such a point that all he wanted to see was the boy's head on a pike. He scoffed and quickly sheathed his sword before mounting his horse with a little effort. "You have not seen the last of me. I shall return." He galloped off and the mother and son watched him disappear into the distance.

"We shall have to report this to the sheriff, otherwise we shall have no defence against any action that we are required to take against that monster," said Aaron to his mother as she stepped in beside him.

Later that same night the mother and son commenced to prepare for slumber when they heard a knock on the door of their house. They quickly stopped what they were doing and listened carefully, listening for any sign as to who it might be.

"Who is it?" asked the mother finally.

"The sheriff, I am here on business," came the steady reply. It was clear that the man on the other side of the door was making an effort to change the sound of his voice.

Aaron looked to his mother and shook his head for he was familiar with the sheriff's voice. "Just a minute," said Aaron in reply. "I am undressed and will be with you shortly."

He picked the crossbow from the wall and smoothly placed a quarrel in place upon the weapon. He nodded to his mother in the little light given off by the lantern, to unbolt the door for the knight to enter. She did so at arm's length and as the door came bursting open Aaron let loose with the quarrel. It was a blur to the eye, the shot of a lifetime, but the agony upon the face of the knight was one that would remain with them for the rest of their lives. He stood there, hunched over, both hands going to the aid of his wound, fingers wrapped around the shaft of the arrow that was now sticking out of his belly. His eyes were wide with shock and pain. The knight fell backwards through the open door, upon the floor, dead.

"We will be arrested for this," said the mother.

"No, it was in self-defence, and the sheriff was advised earlier of this man's evil doings."

"It does nptt matter, son. He has high status," said the mother, concerned.

"No man of high status does as he was going to do," came Aaron's reply. "We shall advise the sheriff in the morning, for now we must get some sleep."

"Do you think I can sleep with a dead man on my doorstep?"

"I shall move the body. But the sheriff must be advised in the morning."

The sheriff rode in beside Aaron, the sheriff upon his horse and Aaron upon the knights. Aaron rode it well and the sheriff noted this. Here beside him was a peasant on a knight's mount, riding along as though born in the saddle. The horrors of the day before were a memory that would be with him forever and a day, especially for his mother who was frail of mind and always concerned for her only son.

"You ride well, Aaron. Is this your first time upon a warhorse?"

"It is, sheriff," replied Aaron. "Why, am I doing something wrong?"

"No, not at all," said the sheriff, but he was lying and lying well. He held the smirk well from his face for Aaron looked as though he was trying to put command to a disobedient donkey.

A little more silence was confronted by both men as they continued towards the farm, the house coming to view on the horizon just a few minutes' ride away. The sun was high in the sky and it was fairly warm, a fresh breeze blowing in from the west.

"I see that you are still troubled," said the sheriff, picking up on the discomfort portrayed within Aaron's voice, noting the way in which he looked off into the distance.

"I am troubled by the grief it has brought my mother. She is fragile, particularly since the death of my father just last year," said Aaron. "She fears that there will be trouble, that I may be arrested for the death of the knight."

"You have nothing to fear, Aaron. You gave notification of the knight's demeanour earlier on. That's all the defence you need.

There will not be any conviction."

"Will you tell my mother that?" asked Aaron. "It will instil confidence within her. It's what she needs right now."

"I shall, Aaron, I shall indeed. And further still I tell you more. The horse you ride no longer has an owner. You would do well to keep the horse, and far be it for me to say, but if I were you I would also keep the knight's mail and weapons. I know the idea might not appeal to you right now, but in a few years... why do you not just put his items of worth away, store them for the future. They will be worth much to any merchant that comes by this way. I shall even write you a note of possession so that none can say that you stole them."

"You are kind, sheriff."

"You deserve the spoils of the knights, in particular from one so filled with the devil." And Aaron thought upon it for a short time. He would store the items away, far from his mother's prying eyes, and one day he would use the possessions to his advantage. And that night he had a dream that surmounted all dreams. He dreamt of knighthood and conviction, of honour and strength, of courage and belief. He loved his mother dearly but hated working upon the farm. His mother was growing old and easily fell ill, in particular during winter. So it was written, there would come a time when the peasant would become a knight, a Knight of the Hospital, to serve mankind as best he could.

He was, in thought alone, a peasant no more.

Four

Tu ne cede malis, sed contra audentior ito

Lars had soon found himself in an inn, a tavern which had gained his immediate attention, and entered without second thought, his crossbow carried in his left hand, quarrels sheathed in a quiver behind his shoulder. It had been a long time since a drop of liquor had passed his lips and all that he cared to do was partake of a small measure to warm his weary bones. He knew that there was plenty of time before the enemy boat could pull into safe harbour, and knew in all realistic terms that he had plenty of time to share with a tankard of full-bodied mead. He entered the premises and Aaron followed close behind, the murky, dark surrounds coming slowly to view as lanterns lit the way for them both.

The smell from within struck them both hard for they were used to the freshness of the sea breeze, not the pissed on floor and beverage-drenched bar, tables and chairs. There was little to no fresh air to speak of in the small tavern, except what managed to find its way in when the door was opened, allowing patrons in and out.

Lars approached to make a purchase, pushing past a few that were seated, one man getting up from his seat as Lars made way to quench his thirst.

"Damn you, old man. Watch where you step," said the rasped voice of the once seated form of a man, well accustomed to strong drink, his iron throat giving way to a deep and threatening groan.

Lars turned to look at the tall man of scarred features and beard and announced without further ado his apology, "Ooo,

ooo."

The man stood silent for a split second and then burst out into bouts of laughter, bending over as though in pain, his comrades, all three, soon joining in on the action. What they saw in front of them was an old man who had taken too much of a liking to rum, having drunk so much in his life that his voice had escaped him completely. Was he a fool or simply drunk out of his mind? A man, who could not speak, could not ask for a drink.

Aaron put his sword hand onto the man's shoulder, seeing a little misunderstanding pass over all four. Who were they to know of Lars' courage, of the work that he had achieved upon the walls of Constantinople, the prowess of his sword work when in the company of other Teutonic Knights.

"Please forgive my captain, for he has no tongue," said Aaron with the sincerest of looks upon his face.

With that spoken all of the men continued laughing uncontrollably, and the one that was standing asked a question to incite further fun and jocularity. "Your captain! You mean to say you follow the orders of a twit who speaks of 'Oooooo'?" the sailors four were having a grand time at someone else's expense, treating a hero with as much disrespect as they could muster.

The group could not contain themselves and others in the tavern looked on from their places, not understanding what the commotion was about and suddenly, without further ado, Aaron had withdrawn his sword from his sheath. The noise died immediately and the stranger who stood stepped back, pulling his sword from a wooden scabbard, a short sword which was no match for Aaron's carver of flesh. The silence that filled the room that minute could be cut with a dagger.

The bar wench also stopped cleaning the tumbler she held in her hands and watched in anxious wait for something to happen, even though the last thing she wanted was a fight amongst her patrons. She had seen enough blood spilt upon the floor of the tavern to know that little business was to be gained from such pitiful affairs. Fighting never amounted to anything but a mess which had to be cleaned up.

"Please, good men, I shall not take well to anyone who spoils this day," said the woman with much confidence but little command, for the two men with swords drawn were ready to throw each other into a melee where there could be only one victor.

"One minute I am minding my own business and the next I am being pushed around for no good reason!" Shouted the offended man with a beard. "He has drawn a sword against me."

"For your cowardly way," voiced Aaron.

The stalemate was not to last long and within just a few short breaths the next stage of the confrontation was to take place: and now for action or in-action, for the man had been shown up in front of his friends. If he fought then he could save face, if he did nothing, he would be frowned upon.

"This man has also shamed me!" said the sailor, looking around to all of those that were seated, in particular to the three men that sat at his table. He could not afford to lose face amongst his friends, for steady friends in the dark of a tavern were hard to come by, unless you were used to buying drinks.

The bar wench spoke further, "I shall shame you too, Martin, if you should not sit yourself down this minute, and I shall ban you from my premises, do you hear?"

"Your husband shall hear of this, that is what I know. Who are you to tell me what to do?" said Martin, who did not take his eyes off the strangers.

"My husband will have to sleep with another if he wants pleasure tonight; do you think he is as stupid as you?"

"I wish an apology from this man who dares draw a sword against me," continued Martin, refusing to allow the situation to simmer, for he had much to lose.

Lars grabbed Aaron by the left arm, "Ooo," and shook his head. This was neither the time nor the place for causing alarm amongst a town which they did not know. How many soldiers were there in town, how many under the arm of the law, ready to bring any undesirable under total control? They could not afford to push the situation further afield. They must apologise.

"My captain advises me against action today, so you can consider yourself in good fortune." And as Aaron went to sheath his weapon, Martin drew his sword arm backwards and prepared to kill the Hospitaller. Suddenly, and in quick as a flash, Lars reached up and behind his shoulder, grasped an arrow and thrust it down into the chest of Martin.

The man screamed and all others remained seated, silent and struck dumb, such speed and unfamiliar action being witnessed. Lars let go of the arrow and it remained in place. The sailor known as Martin dropped his sword and went to the aid of his wound.

"Ah, you filth monger, you have tried to kill me." He pulled the arrow from its mark, throwing it to the floor. Blood started to flow freely from the wound but quickly brought under control by the placement of his right palm. He stepped back and picked up his sword with his left hand and sheathed it. Aaron and Lars noted that his left hand was not his master hand and allowed him the opportunity to place his weapon away, content in the knowledge that no further action was going to take place.

Aaron looked the man in the eye, then at his friends, and to Martin again. "If my good captain wished to kill you, you would be dead. Please consider yourself lucky, for your life has been spared you this day."

"I shall have the sheriff informed," sobbed Martin as he continued to hold his wound with an open palm upon his chest, "and you will be gaoled. You have attacked me without provocation and justice will be served. I have witnesses."

Aaron looked around at the silence and then to the bar wench. "It was in self-defence," said he to all that were listening. "You all could see how this man attempted to attack me openly with his drawn weapon."

"Aye, I saw the whole thing," said the bar wench, who wanted nothing more than to draw a quick and final conclusion to the current unrest. She was in the business of making money, not to give a man the opportunity to spill blood over her tavern's floor

27

at every moment that he stepped through the door.

"I have been coming here for many years now, have I not?" asked Martin. "Does that not count for something? Surely the money I have spent here over the years will be sufficient enough to provide some consolation."

The bar wench again stopped what she was doing. "You are no longer welcome here. Again I say, the company you provide me and the others has expired and you are no longer welcome; I have a reputation to keep," she said. "If you come here again then it will be with an apology of your own. I will not allow blood to be spilled in my tavern; not upon its floors, tables, or anywhere else, which includes at the door."

"And of my friends?"

"They may stay or go, 'tis for them to decide."

Martin looked and half pleaded with his comrades, a final effort on his behalf to try and save face, to pry his comrades from their seats, to get them on his side once more.

"Will you not come with me, leave this dump for what it is; there are plenty of other places for which to get a drink."

"Then go," said one of the seated, "for we have all had enough of your company. You insult many and console few; you have a character of which we all grow tired." And with those words spoken, Martin did depart.

Aaron and Lars gave a silent nod to the seated three and continued to the bar. They were happy to see that Martin was no longer a threat to their presence. They could easily tell that the other three men did not wish to cause any further alarm.

Five

Tu ne cede malis, sed contra audentior ito

Stephen led Bernard and Lambert up the cobbled way as the sky commenced to turn dark, lightning striking the earth with the loudest of cracks and illuminating the area with instantaneous bright light; the storm was upon them. There was a little hail to commence the cracking of thunder above their heads but this soon subsided. They had no time to consider finding shelter for the task they had set themselves, to be completed as soon as possible. The chest of secrets needed to reach its destiny, a house of relatively large proportion that only Stephen knew, and as they continued on their way the cobbled road turned to dirt and the dirt turned to mud. "If we are lucky we shall escape the storm undamaged," said Stephen, "regardless of blinding wind and hail," for he had the foresight to see the things to come, but had not yet mastered his visions completely. They were like moving pictures inside his head, some were blurred and others as clear as day.

"How far, Stephen?" asked Bernard, growing concerned for their wellbeing, for the storm was dampening his faith in the miracles to be unearthed. It was understandable, in the current climate, that such doubt should exist, for they had all suffered much in the voyage from Káros to Barcelona. The sea they had battled on a weekly basis, coming under the threat of being sunk on more than one occasion. It was only through sheer will and courageous effort that they had survived the long trip in such a small boat.

"Not far," answered Stephen without disturbing his stride towards his destination. "We shall be at the house soon enough.

Father Ambaedian has lodging in a reformed school not so far from here, a home now for old sailors with nothing more to do with their time than to drink and be merry. Father Tourmede shared much with me in the little time we had together." He reflected momentarily on the priest from Káros and what he had to say of Father Ambaedian. "But it is not all from the father that I can be grateful, for I can see a picture of the house within my head, as though I have seen it a hundred times."

Bernard questioned Stephen's third eye, "How can you be sure? How do you know that what you see is the house that we are looking for?"

And continuing without turning back to look at the two men carrying the chest Stephen answered, "Because the Lord has provided me with a gift, and although I am learning to use it, it has not yet let me down. I must follow my vision as though it is a map that I hold within my hand. It is not far, we must continue on as best we can. Time is not on our side."

The wind commenced to grow, a thunder clap being heard, and hail, like tiny stones, fell once more from the sky once more, but only briefly; and they were thrashed. Bernard and Aaron held their free hand over the face as they continued and Stephen said unto himself, 'and the way will be molested by thrashing grains'.

"It comes from nowhere," yelled Lambert above the noise of the storm. "Never before have I witnessed such a squall as this. It must be something that the devil has created." Stephen fell into stride beside the two men with chest, failing to have heard correctly what Lambert had said.

"And where do you think such a storm comes?" questioned Stephen.

"I hate to admit, but lie I cannot; I see the Lord laughing down upon us, teaching us a lesson for something we have done, or are about to do. Either that or the devil has laid command over the skies and is trying to delay us for one reason or another."

"You fail to see Him as I do, Lambert; for the Lord has made this storm from nothing and for good reason."

"And for what reason, may I ask?"

"For the storm would have reached its worse long before the brigantine would have had the chance to moor. The storm is our salvation. God is protecting us from those of Muslim faith. He is providing us with the time we need to get us to our destination."

Six

Tu ne cede malis, sed contra audentior ito

The story of Martin.

The battle had been won, they were successful. The songs of victory were carried upon the wind and across the battlefield for all to hear, the last of the slain laying with their heathen comrades upon the desert ocean, upon the carpet of red that now dominated the area. The dead lay upon the field like locusts cover a crop, where a man cannot walk from one side of the battlefield to the other without falling over a corpse. Dead horses were laying upon men, men upon horses; where you saw one you saw the other, each blending in to form one miserable sight, a mass of slaughter, enough to bring vomit to the lips of anyone that lived.

Martin was a young soldier, a man who had the full intention of becoming more than just a follower; he wanted to be a leader of men, or at least amongst those that were considered as elite. He had ability and strength, courage and skill. But now... he was sickened by the slaughter. He had finally had enough. His station within the desert was a hard one, but boring to say the least. Sure, a few battles here and there lifted his spirits slightly, but he had not yet, until this day, felt that he had served the Lord as the Lord should be served. But this, it was the battle of all battles; it went beyond the call to service.

He was kneeling, slumped beside one of the last to die, a Muslim with a thick line of hair upon his upper lip and a week's growth upon his chin. He had been skewered well by Martin, who himself had been wounded in the upper left arm. The wound was not deep but very painful, pain which was only now beginning to take hold, for before now the adrenalin had been pumping so ferociously throughout his body that it was even hard to control his action, even minutely so. He had fought well, taking his opponents one at a time, defeating each as they fell upon him, the Turk doing all he could to take his life as Martin did all he could to protect it.

His commander drew up alongside the man under his command, on foot and scouring the battlefield to check on the victory, looking for wounded enemy to torture and friendly soldiers that might need medical attention.

"I know you by name, do I not? Martin I believe."

"That is correct, sir. I am Martin."

"Are you alright? Can you walk?"

"I can, sir, I can walk from here to the end of the earth for any task, if such a task is worth the effort," said Martin, the sadness of his voice coming to air.

"You sound defeated, somewhat lacking in spirit," said the commander. "Are you hurt badly? Are you tired?"

"I am tired, sir, that is the answer," and Martin turned to look up to the man looking down upon him. "I am tired of the killing and this sodden desert. I thought I wanted more, to serve the Lord by slaying his enemy." Martin had had enough. There was no more to experience in life but death itself. "But I have had enough of the heat and the flies, the maggots and stale bread. If there was a purpose to the death and slaughter then I could live with it, but this is insane."

"You speak of treason, Martin. I would calm my voice down if I were you. You will get yourself a field punishment if you are not careful of what you say, and be careful of whom you say it in front of." The commander relaxed on his verbal assault and looked over the battlefield briefly, seeing wounded men getting up from their knees, picking up their swords, dragging a dagger across the throat of some of the wounded. "There is much slaughter here today, I must see to it that no more wounded are killed before they have been properly interrogated, but please, tell me, what is it that will tend to your... wounds? What will bring you comfort?"

Martin looked to his commander and stood up, coming eye to eye, and speaking his whole hearted truth he said to his commander, "I wish to be provided another station. I hear that the Hospital is seeking recruits. It is here that I wish to serve, to be charitable instead of blood thirsty. If there is the slightest hope that I can do more for mankind than I currently do then I must do it. Look around you, sir. What do you see? Slaughter to the likes that no man should witness, and what for? A station within the desert, a small outpost that serves nobody, not even the pilgrims that travel to this holy land. Yes, it is the holy land. It is here that I must serve. I must serve the people as the people serve us. They till the land and grow the crops; they feed this great army and feed us well. The commerce of our homeland is supplied by the peasants of our country, and how do we thank them? I do not see the point in fighting over a few yards of blood-soaked desert, nor in the downfall of Islam unless it pays us well by bringing belief and honour to us all."

"Belief and honour," said the commander. "Do you honestly believe there is no honour in what we do? We serve the Lord by bringing death to the heathen. They are sacrilegious devils who do not deserve to draw a single breath of air as provided by God."

"I am sorry, sir, but I have had enough. I cannot kill any more unless such killing is in the defence of something righteous; I cannot and will not. Do you not see the lack of purpose? There is no good will in what we do."

The commander looked again over the field of slaughter, taking the view in, like he had not done before. He reflected momentarily on the dead and dying, of the good cause of what had been achieved.

"Victory is ours, that is achievement enough," said the commander. "But I recall a little of the service you have paid, of your honour and duty bound moralistic servitude. I shall grant you what you wish. I shall call you to a meeting later. When you are called then you must come." His commander turned to depart but stopped and faced him one more time. "It would be wise to keep your opinions to yourself, for others will not look upon you with the favour I am about to bestow."

Martin was called into the tent as it stood upon the sands of the desert, one of many that had been erected not far from the battlefield, an administrational city of tents. The commander was seated before him, and next to him sat a priest. The priest was dressed in the regalia of a knight of the Hospital. He was not a big man, as he was prone to pray rather than to fight. A large cross hung around his neck on a thick chain; a bible sat before him upon the small table, slightly to the side but within easy reach.

"Martin, This man beside me is Father Alfred, he runs a sacred mission in the Aegean Sea, not far from Greece, but far from conflict."

Martin looked at the man with a nod of his head, "Good afternoon, father."

"I am happy to meet you, my son," said the priest. "I have been advised that you grow sour at the killing and wish to be tested with something more worthy. I also hear that court martial looms on the wind for one such as yourself, but I have been advised," and with that spoken looked to Martin's commander with acknowledgment, "that you are indeed worthy of the good right, the right to be recruited into an arm of the Order of the Hospital that I believe will serve you well. Yes, it will serve you well as you must serve it." The priest sat back relaxed before continuing. "There is not much fighting where I come from, but there is plenty of prayer. There is no bloodshed, no pilgrims, no horses or other beasts restricted by collar; but there is still plenty of work to be done."

Martin could not believe his ears. He had come so close to execution for his sour words that he could barely believe what he was hearing. "Why would you, father, wish to help one like me, who should be nothing more than a condemned man? Why should I be worthy of your presence at such a time as this?"

"Let me simply say that I serve the Lord as I believe you wish to serve. I have many ears and in many camps. Many men carry my sacred banner, which is to justify each man's existence, never to condemn anyone without good cause. If you can serve better, elsewhere, then who am I to turn a blind eye? If you can serve charitably then you should be given that opportunity."

Martin looked coolly from his commander to the priest. Here before him was his saviour. At present it appeared too good to be true, but it all sounded very adventurous. If it was true, and his commander was indeed the eyes and ears of the priest, it stood to good reason that the priest knew exactly who he was getting to serve him. To serve in the Order renowned for its charity, to serve the Lord, and further still, to serve in a special arm of the Order of the Hospital.

"Father Alfred," said Martin, "I shall not let you down."

"That is to be seen, my son," said the priest, "but I believe my eyes and my heart. I am an old man but not without my brains and ability to think clearly. I know a good man when I see one." The priest picked up the bible and passed it to Martin, who took it up in his hands. "This is your ticket. It is a special book and will be recognised by certain members of our staff. Any of our Order will recognise it. You can show it as required on your journey to Káros. The book will give you free passage and enough food to relieve your hunger. With this book comes your salvation into an Order that cannot be spoken amongst strangers or friends. You must not tell others of this meeting here today. I shall see you in Káros within the fortnight of your arrival. You may go now."

Martin stood with the book in his hand. "Thank you, father," he said. "I shall go with as much speed as I can muster."

 *Seven*

Tu ne cede malis, sed contra audentior ito

"Quickly, in here," shouted the nun against the wind which rattled the thick-set door upon its hinges as it was opened. A little rain stung at her face, the storm commencing to grow more ferocious as each minute in time passed them by, a little flooding and damage to buildings the obvious outcome, for none had witnessed such a storm in all their life. If the storm continued as it was then the town folk were in for a hard weekend. "Come children, as quickly as you can, before you are drenched to the bone."

As the children passed through the door, Martin stood to one side. "Thank you, Sister."

"Later, my son," she said whilst looking over the group of children, seeing their appalling condition, drenched to the bone and dressed in near rags. "Get the children to the fire, quickly now."

The children were gathered around the open fire place of the large hall. Martin and Raoul looked around the den of hope, Lois and Catherine standing before them. "Go and join the other children, you are as they are, orphans," said Martin. The child named Catherine did not budge but just stood there, looking at the two men as though each were a commander in chief.

"We are more than that," said Catherine. "We are one and the same with Stephen. He is our Lord and master.

"This is not a game, child," added Raoul. "Until we hear from Stephen himself we must stay here and abide by the house rules, and... ah, Sister." He flicked Catherine aside with fingers, flapping them in front of her face, hoping she would do as she was directed, to take the nun's prying eyes away from her.

"Good evening... well, not that grand, but our fire will keep you warm for the time being. I am Sister Bardwell. There are five of us here. The others are tending to the children of the orphanage at this time," the Sister looked down upon Catherine who had taken a few steps back. "You may go child, join the others. A bowl of soup will be served soon."

"Yes, Sister, thankyou," and the child was happy with the invitation that had reached her ears, for a good bowl of hot soup had not passed her lips for so very long.

"Thirteen children and an escort of two," Sister Bardwell added as Catherine joined the others around the fireplace, Lois coming up to stand at her side. "From where do you come?"

"Far from here, Sister," said Martin. "We commenced our journey from Constantinople."

"Oh, what is the news?"

"It has fallen."

"Oh, my dear Lord. Such a crime against the church this is. All of those poor souls." Sister Bardwell looked to both the men, seeing for the first time their dress. "I see you are armed sailors. Tell me; did they suffer? Did many escape?"

"Many boats filled with souls did make it into the Aegean and beyond but many more were slaughtered under the long arm of Mehmet and his criminals. We were lucky to make it out," lied Martin, for he was from Káros, not Constantinople, but their masquerade must be maintained. "Some fled to Pera, some were cut off in withdrawal. But that is of little consequence now. We have these children, Sister. They need to be cared for until such a time that our master can return with news."

"Master? News of what?"

"The children will be delivered to a safe haven not too far from here, but such accommodation cannot be secured without our master's approval," said Raoul. "He does not intend to provide the children with a home unless such can accommodate them as they should be accommodated."

"So you do not wish to deliver these children to this orphanage?" she looked around the room they were in. "A convent it is but we tend to children's needs like any good Christian. But what of the children; they are to become... what exactly?"

"They are to be educated and housed in a school that only our master knows. He shall return within a few days, certainly no longer than a few weeks," said Raoul. There was also the situation with money, for they had none. "But, Sister, we cannot pay, but work we can."

"Work, ah. Well, there is plenty of that to go around. I shall introduce you to the Mother Superior after the children have partaken of their breakfast in the morning and you two gentlemen have had time to dry yourselves in front of the fireplace, and sufficiently rested."

"Thank you, Sister. Your charity is most humbly accepted."

"Not at all. Now, I shall attend to something for you and the children to eat, after which I shall leave you two gentlemen till morning breaks," and with that said she disappeared through one of the four doorways connected to the main hall.

Later that night the Sister approached the Mother Superior and advised her of the two men and thirteen children. The Mother Superior's mind, being an administrator, counsellor, and servant of God, never stopped in its processing of information. What she had heard the Sister speak of did not entirely make her at ease with the situation. It seemed quite unrealistic that such a master, as the one the two men spoke of, should have the need to venture further in land in an endeavour to secure a home for thirteen orphans so far from Constantinople. There seemed to be very little planning and many errors in the scenario that had been painted for her: why did they decide not to stop at another port? Why travel so far? She would dwell on it all tonight; consider, with much thought, everything that had been disclosed to her, for the children's future was most important.

Eight

Tu ne cede malis, sed contra audentior ito

A man seemingly drunk and half mad burst through the door of the inn. The wind and torrential rain followed his entry into the comfort of the premises. All heads and eyes turned to the scene as the man attempted to shut the door behind him.

"Close that door, damn you," cried the bar wench, for the wind was strong and made the candles flicker with unease, the coldness of the night rolling through the air thick with smoke, striking at the faces of those partaking of beverage.

"Aye," the sailor complied with much effort, and with the door finally shut he turned his attention to those that looked on in bewilderment. "The storm rages. Many boats are being smashed to smithereens. There is no escaping it."

"Come here and buy a drink," insisted the bar wench, eager to make another sale.

"Aye; sounds inviting," said the man as he licked his lips and made out with quick stride towards the wench as she poured him a tumbler of her finest.

Aaron looked to Lars. "I think it's time we departed, to see for ourselves what the storm had brought us." Lars nodded in agreement.

Aaron looked at the woman. "Thankyou for the warmth you so nobly provided us, but we must commence our journey."

"In this weather?" asked a drunken sod, ease-dropping in the conversation. "You are fools. I just witnessed the true horrors of the sea; there is no escaping it," his eyes were as round as pieces of gold.

Aaron slapped a coin upon the counter and the sailor eyed it greedily.

"I see you are well endowed," he said.

"We look after ourselves as we see fit, and with our thirst quenched we shall retire and seek shelter. But first we must see to our boat, see whether she is still moored safety upon the pier or not"

"Here," said the bar wench. "Nothing wrong with my place, is there? I have plenty of room and board, rooms for the likes that the king of any country would be happy to spend the night."

"A most deserving premise, I am sure, but my companion and I must seek out our friends," added Aaron. "We thank you for the information."

"Well come back soon, and bring your friends; so long as no tab is sought for what you should drink." And with that Lars and Aaron stepped from the counter and towards the door, the offer of room and board tucked deep in their heads, for they might well desire to change their mind.

"Work, work I seek," said a drunkard sailor, grabbing onto Aaron's sleeve.

"We have no time and little to pay," said Aaron as he attempted to move past the sailor, grabbing the man's hand and pushing it aside.

"A coin would do you well to pay, for I have something for you," said the sailor, a twinkle in his eyes appearing as he looked into Aaron's face directly.

Aaron and Lars looked at the man and decided to listen, for they were new in town and could do with all the help they could muster. "Speak quickly for our time is short," said Aaron, seemingly displeased that his departure had been disturbed.

"I wonder," teased the sailor, "if your arm might be long enough to find something for me in your dark and deep pocket?" for the promise of coin was a subject most favoured.

"If what you speak pleases me then you shall be given your just reward."

The sailor looked around, left and right. "A man hides amongst the shadows, to the left as you exit the inn, well out of storm's way he cowers. Saw him with my own eyes, I did. Very suspicious that one, standing there like a statue, not bothering to find better shelter from the storm and cold air."

Aaron smiled. "And does this man have a sword sheathed or ready for action."

"Ready for action, as far as I could tell," said the sailor holding out an open palm, hoping for it to be filled with a just reward.

Aaron reached into his pocket and withdrew a coin for the drunkard. "Take this as your payment for services rendered," and the sailor went to turn tail. "But before you spend what you have been provided, listen to me closely."

The sailor came close, head hung to the left. "What is it?"

"We shall be in town for a few days; your help would be rewarded in the future as it is today."

"Thank you, kind friend, I shall keep my eyes open for you; and my name is John." Both knights smiled, and then Aaron and Lars made for the door.

Nine

Tu ne cede malis, sed contra audentior ito

Abu could not believe his luck, which to date was secured through his cunning ways and masterful skills as seaman and commander; but this storm was whipped from nothing, grew from a pleasant breeze to a deadly gale in minutes, cloud as dark as the darkest of nights covering the sky in what seemed to be seconds. So close to harbour they were, to moor their stolen vessel upon European soil, to mingle with the Latin of this land, to pursue the chest of secrets. Never before had he seen or heard of such terror as that which they now experienced, and suddenly, out of nowhere, a wave as freakish as a mental woman with pointed nails, came crashing down upon them. Their masts were snapped like twigs from a dead tree, many men crushed as they fell upon the deck, others were washed overboard to drown in the Mediterranean, and so close to shore. It was the wrath of God, but why? And as suddenly as that question pierced his mind, lightning struck at the ship in several places, catching it on fire.

Men ran here and there, but with no sails to aid them they were dead in the water, crippled and unable to steer, unable to defend against the hail, wind, and fury. Their boat continued to close the gap between themselves and the moored vessels of Barcelona, the harbour so close that they could almost touch it, and with the closing-of-the-gap came the look of terror within each of the sailor's eyes for they were heading on a collision course with a singular rock formation that jutted out from the sea near the entrance to the coastal city. Like a sentry, this pinnacle of rock seemed to be stationed for a single purpose, as though planted there for a reason; their destruction.

Sailor's screamed orders, messages passed from one to the other, but none were heard or acted upon; it was every man for himself. Men clambered over the fallen masts of the ship, trying with such great effort to escape the horrors of the night, the thrashing sea, and the torment of the fire that was not contained by the rain, for it shrugged off all restraint. The boat moved with the sea, up and down, side to side, the hull being hit hard by wave after wave, a beating which did not cease.

Suddenly they crashed into the rock formation, the bow breaking and letting a torrent of water into the hold. Men jumped frantically from the deck and into the waters of the Mediterranean, so close to land but so far, for even the best of swimmers – which were few – had trouble breaking the surface of the sea as they swam for their lives. It was a miracle in itself that anyone could muster the power to swim in the storm, but a handful made their way to shore and upon their minds they knew why they had suffered, for Abu had ordered that they refrain from prayer, to put their religion behind them. Their commander was to blame for their demise; he solely had condemned them to death. This was their punishment for their individual heinous act against their god, refusing to pay homage where homage should be paid. And to those that made the shore; they looked upon their delivery from hell as a gift from God, and to Him they silently prayed. God had saved them, but what of the others? God had not saved anything but a handful. And of all the men that were boarded upon the stolen vessel only five had survived; Abu, Ahmad, Ibrahim, Mollet, and Sherif. And not a single one of them could understand how it was they, Abu's favourites, that had survived the ordeal at sea. How was it possible that a handful of chosen could escape death when everyone else did succumb to the power of nature at its worst. It was as though written, but this is the way the thrown dice had landed. A coincidence, was after all, just a coincidence. Was it possible that having been together at the time of the disaster, saved them all, by the choicest of thrashing waves delivering them to safety.

They alone had made it to shore and were thankful for their lives having been spared. And as they crawled upon the beach, being thrashed continuously by waves, they managed to get far enough from the waters of the Mediterranean in order to catch their breath, but they had no time to waste, no time to rest where they lay.

They each stood and looked out upon the sea, looking for their boat, but it could not be seen.

Aaron stepped out into the cold and slash of hail first, his sword drawn and held vertical in front of his body, and just as well, for the shadows revealed the man in wait, who's slashing sword was parried easily by Aaron, and as quickly as the two swords struck, the cowardly man did run off into hiding. Aaron simply watched on as the figure of a man disappeared into the dark of the night.

Aaron laughed out loud, "It seems as though a fledgling has fled to fight another day." Lars pulled on Aaron's sleeve to grasp his attention. Lars pointed off into the distance as the boats within the harbour smashed against one another. Their carrack could not be seen, having been sunk quickly, taken in by the hungry sea. Anything that they wanted from on board would now be denied them. They both looked at the empty mooring where their boat had been put to rest. They did not know it had sunk, simply thought it had been stolen, taken by the harbour master or one of his accomplices. It was clear to them, from the lack of what they saw, that the harbour master was to be held responsible, but they could not be concerned over it at present, for other more meaningful tasks awaited their undivided attention. Aaron looked Lars in the eye. "I once heard a Wiseman say that no one should be burdened by heavy possession." He sheathed his sword.

Lars then led the way and Aaron followed, keeping his head up and looking around, seeking the dark of shadows for those that might be in wait as they headed for the harbour. They approached quickly and saw in the distance, and just in time, the enemy ship as she sank, the brigantine being swallowed up by the sea around it. Closer to shore, a few sailors' heads could be seen bobbing up and down amongst the waves before they disappeared, and there, not too far away, a few persons had dragged themselves out of the sea, onto a formation of rock and sand that was being washed by the waters of the Meditteranean. It could be none other than those that had been chasing them these past months.

Lars in particular could not believe his luck, for the enemy had been delivered into his hand. He saw this as nothing less than a great opportunity. They had never locked eyes upon one another before, but who else could it be that would be swimming amongst the waves of this powerful storm, if not from the sunken brigantine. He shook the sleeve of Aaron and pulled him, and headed towards the flank of the pier where normally would be found a beach of pearl, white sand. They ran as fast as they could, their angle of sight no longer allowing them to see the bodies of the men now washed ashore, and no sooner had the Muslims themselves been beached upon the sandbars of Barcelona, and looked out upon the surface of the sea, then they rushed for cover beneath the pier some distance away to gather themselves some courage and shelter from the storm, the thrashing waves continuing, bashing against their thighs from time to time, the waves rolling in and out with great force. The shelter of the pier would provide immediate cover from the rain but not the sea, and also provide them the time to make plans for their next move.

Meanwhile, Lars and Aaron moved closer towards the underbelly of the pier, unable to see clearly in the storm and shadow, unable to consider their enemy in wait. They stepped well clear of the waves as best they could, as each crashed themselves upon the shore, each of the men wading no deeper than their upper thighs at any given time. They were currently side by side, straining to see clearly into the shadows formed of the pier, where the higher ground and built up dune of sand provided for easier movement and less wave.

"They will be tired from the swim ashore," said Aaron to Lars.

"You stay here, Lars, and I will move towards them; try to flush them out. Be ready with your crossbow, for it is our only advantage."

"Ooo," agreed Lars, preparing a quarrel, placing it upon his weapon of choice. Aaron moved towards the space beneath the pier, the hail having subsided, but the stinging rain continued unabated. He caught a glimpse of something, the metal blade of a sword, a little twinkle of light from the stars above had been handed a temporary reprieve from their concealment above the clouds, just enough for Aaron to be advantaged by the grace of God. The knight stopped, just yards separating him from the hidden.

"Come out so that I may see you," Aaron was brave and particularly mindful of Lars, who stood some distance behind, upon a small rock and with his crossbow ready with quarrel. "We seek to know who has followed us these many miles, to see for ourselves who dares—"

Mollet leapt like a startled gazelle from beneath the pier as the other four withdrew out of the other side, his sword held in two hands above his head, slicing down in action to deliver a deadly blow upon Aaron. The scream from Mollet struck Aaron hard, but the scream soon fell into silence, Mollet's body struck hard by an arrow from Lars, and the downward thrust of his sword missed Aaron by mere inches as the body fell to the ground. Mollet had been slain with as much ease as one scratches an irritating itch.

Aaron let out with a great exhale and rushed into the darkness, and as the pier's shadow covered him from view, Lars' dashed forward to stand by his friend's side, shifting his crossbow into position behind his back as he moved, pulling his sword from its sheath in preparation for further action.

Lars drew alongside Aaron who simply looked out from beneath the pier, "Gone but not forgotten. They have gotten away, Lars. I could not see them clearly as they would have seen me, and you with your crossbow will be hard to miss in a crowd. Maybe you should consider leaving it here," for he was much concerned for their safety, in particular when their surroundings were so unfamiliar.

Lars shook his head. Although he had a sword, as any other man would have, he dare not part with his third arm, the crossbow and the quarrels that fed it.

"I think we should gain shelter from this foul weather. Do you feel up to going back to the tavern so humble?"

Lars nodded acceptance.

"Let us take turns in sleeping tonight; I do not trust room-and-board when so many enemies are prowling about, but at least we know that a room can be gained from the tavern, even if just for the night."

Abu waited for the others to gather amongst the shadows of the buildings surrounding them, the rain was dissipating and the thunder was rolling on, further afield and away from them at long last.

"That stupid Mollet," cursed Abu. "What manner of man tempts to take on a crossbow from such a distance?"

"He was right to do as he did," stated Sherif. "In fact, we should all have rushed the two men. We would have been victorious: if not so worn and tired."

Abu looked at the man in silence and shook his head. "You, all of you are impossible. They knew who we were which means only one thing, they were who we sought, and being the case are needed alive. How are we supposed to find the chest without them? Ibrahim, Ahmad, Sherif: ah; how do we proceed without them?"

"Well, there is no following now," added Ahmad. "The two have gone, lost forever."

"Again, a eunuch when it comes to foresight, and with only one eye in your head to see, Ahmad, you are almost useless to our cause." Abu was tiring of their stupidity. Ahmad rubbed consciously at the scar upon his socket, where his left eye used to be. "The one with the crossbow looks to me to be at one with war. A man of such age and still clinging to a crossbow knows not of peace and sanctity. Find the crossbow and we find the chest."

"Shall we go now and seek the crossbow?" asked Ibrahim.

"No," said Abu. "We shall wait until the weather clears and split into two groups. We shall find them if it takes us all week. I do not care how long it takes in fact; I want that chest in our possession."

Ten

Cu ne cede malis, sed contra audentior ito

The story of Lambert.

Lambert stood guard at the door to Constantine's palace, a great honour of which he was proud to serve. The populace of Constantinople served their emperor with heart and soul; he too served with no less conviction. He was not regarded as having any great wealth in the form of status but his position was much sought after. The privileged station provided much news on the disposition and state of Byzantium as well as regular pay and good food. And where a man was single, as he, a room for the likes that a peasant would kill for was provided, even if it was nothing more than a disused stable, though refurbished for man of flesh.

Lambert had been in the service of Constantine for many years and in that time had journeyed with him into many territories, both those that belonged to Byzantine and those that belonged to the enemy. He was not a stranger to fighting and had drawn his sword on many occasions to fight off an assault directed at his emperor, his sword having spilled much blood during the time he had been assigned to the emperor's personal bodyguard. It was now that his supreme commander and emperor of Constantinople, called for a personal audience with him, man to man, no other present.

Lambert was directed into the dining room where Constantine sat at one end of a long table. Two places had been set, and although not common, the two places set were at right angles, Lambert's seat being on the right of where Constantine sat.

50

Constantine stood and greeted the common soldier as the great wooden doors closed behind him, the personal servant to the emperor stepping backwards as the doors were pulled shut.

"Please, Lambert. Come in and have a seat," said Constantine, his voice calm and without pressure, a soft tone of friendship easily noted.

"Thank you, my Lord," replied Lambert of the invitation.

He drew alongside the table and sat as did Constantine, many platters of food already in place for the private meeting to take place. Several glasses sat empty above where a plate was positioned, empty and waiting to be filled. Bottles of wine were also present, ready to be poured, which the emperor did for them both, filling one of Lambert's glasses first and then his own.

"Lambert, how many years have you served me now?"

"Many, my Lord, at least five, possibly a little more," answered Lambert. "Time goes so fast when you enjoy what you do, my Lord, and serving you has been nothing less than a great honour.

"And how many battles have we been in, you by my side, warding off the enemy when one strayed too close?"

"Too many, my Lord. Much blood has encased my sword. The battles are so many that they cannot be counted with all of my fingers and toes."

"Ah, yes. It is true, Lambert. You have served me so preciously, with your whole hearted attention, with such conviction that you have never been questioned. That is why I have now pressed upon you to dine with me. You, my bodyguard of many years, have served so well. I would now like to try and return the service, so to speak, by providing you with a task that will see you guaranteed a place in heaven."

"Thank you, my Lord," said Lambert, puzzled by the words, concerned that the emperor may be asking too much. "It has always been a pleasure."

"Please, help yourself to whatever you desire, eat like you've never eaten before," and Constantine looked over the set table in all its splendour. "Come, help yourself, and I shall provide you with more detail before this day concludes."

And with a wide smile upon Lambert's face he did help himself to the food laid out in front of him, as did Constantine. They ate festively, commenting on past actions, bringing to memory the battles they had fought in, the close scrapes, and the minor injuries sustained during such actions. And the time came when the food had mostly been eaten, except for a few scraps here and there. They had both had a good fill of food and wine.

"Tell me, Lambert," said Constantine. "Where would you see yourself in a few years?"

"Here, my Lord, beside you, eaten like a hungry pig, getting my fill," said Lambert, smiling and letting go of a hearty laugh, filling the air with happiness and great joy, "for you will be as happy with my services to you as much then as you are now, and then we can eat some more."

This brought an immediate smile to Constantine, a smile to outdo the smile that he had previously worn. He was content, he was happy; he had made the right decision. But the time had arrived, the time to divulge the mission that Lambert was to be given.

"Something is needed, Lambert. I need your services like I have never needed them before. I need you to run an errand for me and once that errand has been achieved I need you to serve another... with no less conviction than you have served me, but with great vigour and all your heart... as I know you will serve."

"My Lord, I will do all that I can to ensure that I serve your every wish. I shall do as you command."

"Well, Lambert, it is not as much as a command. It is a request. You can choose to turn it down if you so desire."

"My Lord, I do not see how I can turn you down. We have been through so much together, that if you believe I am the right man for the job then I will serve like I have never served before."

"I am most pleased to hear that. The task is a simple one but must remain secret."

"Yes, my Lord, a secret."

"It is most serious, Lambert. Even with the threat of torture hanging over your heard you must not relinquish your mission to anyone, and the parcel you carry must be destroyed." Lambert could hear the importance of the mission as the emperor spoke of it. Something so important was to fall his way that his very life could be in danger. He could feel the eyes in the walls of the dining room; he could feel the spies hanging on Constantine's every word. "What is it, my Lord?"

"You will not understand fully, Lambert, but I need you to take a parcel of three books to a Father Tourmede."

"And where do I find such a man?"

Constantine fell silent for a short while and then spoke. "On the island of Káros, in the Aegean Sea."

Eleven

Tu ne cede malis, sed contra audentior ito

The weather continued unabated as Stephen led the other two along the sodden road. The hail was making itself well known, stinging at the body garments of the three, lashing out at their faces as they each tried to hold their arms across their face. Their backs were pelted hard by the storm but still they pushed themselves on into the night.

"How far now?" questioned Lambert as loudly as he possibly could and still remain audible, finding the walking hard though not because of the weight of the chest. He was soaked to the body and could feel the crinkling of his skin as it surrendered to the effects of being drenched.

"Not far," yelled back Stephen. He did not look back at the others but continued on, forcing the two men behind him to step out and maintain their pace.

"That is the third time you have said that," Lambert reminded, for they had been walking for what seemed to be hours.

"Maybe true," replied Stephen as he came to a halt in front of a house. "But this time I speak the truth. Here it is, come, quickly." It was a large building set far aside from others on the road. This was not a town, or even a village. It was nothing more than a few buildings that supported travellers along the road, providing a station for which to rest, refuel, and gather one's strength.

They each headed for the door and Stephen knocked loudly. They waited impatiently, drenched to the skin, the wind chill factor of the weather commencing to take its toll, for Lambert let out with uncontrollable shivering. Stephen knocked again, and again no answer. Lambert and Bernard placed the chest down and Lambert stepped up to the door, trying to gain a little protection from the weather and to try the door for himself. "Third time lucky," he said and knocked as loudly as he could, and within a minute the door opened; just a little at first.

A man in priest's vestment stood in front of them with a smile. He laid eyes upon Stephen and then his two comrades. "Please enter, quickly now," and stepped aside to let the men past, holding the door with all his strength against the wind that pushed upon it.

"Thank you," said Stephen as the three entered a hallway with the chest, their clothes dripping upon the cold stone floor, bright light from an adjoining room spilling out into the hallway, flickering over the walls.

The door was finally closed and bolted from the inside. "Such a terrible day to be walking out," said the priest as he held out his hand. "I am Father Ambaedian."

Father Ambaedian looked behind to ensure the three men followed him into the main hall. It was dark except around the huge fireplace and not a soul to be seen.

"All of the men are asleep in their rooms," Ambaedian's eyes fell upon the chest, "and we will not be disturbed."

Stephen said to the priest, "I see by the look in your eyes that you know what we carry?"

"Indeed," replied Ambaedian. "I know the chest by sight." He shook it from his mind. "Please, set yourselves down and warm yourselves by the fire, I shall get some refreshment for you shortly."

"Thank you, father."

"I have some wine to warm you all, and bread and cheese," said the priest as he watched the men seat themselves, "But first things first. Who are you? I do not recognise any of you."

"I am Stephen, and these two men are knights of the Hospital. I came from Constantinople and these men from Káros."

"Constantinople?"

"Yes, father, and it has fallen. A great loss it is," added

55

Stephen, knowing full well that Father Ambaedian would ask. "I was there for a week only, and saw the fall of the great city for myself. I was lucky to get out alive," and the memory of his wife came flooding back, but he continued nevertheless. "I met Father Norotus who disclosed information to me in regards to the chest and its secret."

"Father Norotus," said Father Ambaedian with reflection in his eye. "I do not recall having ever heard of him. Please, continue."

"Well," continued Stephen, "we sailed to Káros and once there I fell in with these marvellous men. I also spent time with Father Tourmede."

"Ah, so that is why you are here, by his request" interrupted the priest, for he now understood. "How is Father Tourmede?"

Stephen was not sure but refused to lie to Father Ambaedian. "The fortress was attacked by many Turks. We had no choice but to flee. Father Tourmede and several nuns stayed on the island, to hide from the Muslims. They have all honoured themselves, for they gave up their place upon our boat, in order that we could protect thirteen orphans."

"Thirteen orphans?"

"Father, there is much to disclose, it will take a while," said Stephen, prompting the priest to provide further comfort.

"Of course, I'm sorry. Let me gather some refreshment, stoke the fire... and then we can talk further."

Twelve

Tu ne cede malis, sed contra audentior ito

Father Ambaedian entered the hall where the warmth from the huge open fireplace shook the cold from the stone floor, and old and weary limbs. He held a small tray with tumblers of a measured substance, some wine to take further chill from within, some bread and cheese could also be seen.

The priest placed the tray down and the three knights simply looked on as Father Ambaedian handed out the tumblers, the sweetness of the wine hitting their nostrils. "Please drink heartedly and eat well," invited Father Ambaedian. "This wine was made from our own garden, a small measure of land attached to the rear of this house. The sailors we tend to help with the workload and we are always grateful for what they can do to make life easier for us here."

The two Hospitaller drank from their tumblers but Stephen placed his down and by showing his respect did decline the drink by saying, "Thankyou, father, but my mind must remain clear, as I am sure you understand, but your bread and cheese looks marvellous."

The priest was silent for a short second before allowing his thoughts to be heard, contemplating the company that sat before him.

"You will have to forgive me; but may I say as I please in front of your men?" asked Ambaedian, the knights looking each other in the eye.

"These two knights know as much about the chest as I do," said Stephen in reply. "They can be trusted with its contents and are pure; they will not whither, and death will not be delivered unto them if the chest is opened."

"So it is true," said Ambaedian. "If the chest is opened then all those that are impure will be struck as though by lightning – the finger of god?"

"It is indeed true and we have seen many deaths," said Stephen. "I can tell you this; of over one hundred good human beings, only a handful survived the opening of the chest."

"Such power exists?"

"It does."

"How many times has it been opened?" asked the priest.

"Only once, that I can be sure," said Stephen. "We do not know how many times it has been opened before its arrival on Káros, but needless to say it would not have been many. The key and the chest were kept well apart in an endeavour to prevent anyone from releasing the secret to the world, and just as well."

Father Ambaedian was without drink and interlocked his fingers in front of his wiry frame. "I grow old," and with a smile, continued, "and rather frail, but know my destiny. I have studied as much about the chest and its contents as I possibly could these past few decades. The volumes that my finger has traced cannot be counted for there are so many. Verses, phrases, and sentences alike, all have their hidden clues, accusations, and truths. I believe in the Lord our Father and it is for Him that I continue in life as He does in heaven." He fell silent then and asked a question of Stephen. "And what can you tell me of the chest, its markings, and of the secret it holds?" and Stephen delivered to him a verbal account of the contents of the letter from Constantine, information on Father Tourmede and his many volumes of text, and the ceremony of the opening of the chest at Káros, and father Ambaedian was much enthralled.

At this same time Aaron and Lars returned to the inn, which they had left with regret, for its warmth and atmosphere – besides anything to do with the man known as Martin – was something to be embraced on a cold and stormy night. They entered as they did before, all eyes upon them, each and every one wishing to know who was about to enter. A little stunned silence was encountered as the patrons of the tavern looked on before them, seeing without mistake that the two men who had departed in bad tiding had returned, before losing themselves once more in drink and conversation.

Lars and Aaron continued on towards the huge counter and the woman standing behind it, her forearms resting upon it as she learned forward.

"My fair lady," said Aaron to the bar wench. "It is good that your door is still open to the weary, for we are such, and look to rest our bones and flesh from the cold of the night. We would like to take up on your previous offer of a room for the night; or what remains of it."

"I have a room to suit you both, in the attic," she turned to attend the pouring of another tumbler for a customer who leant weatherly against the bar. "There are plenty of blankets to keep you both warm, you can pick them up from the trunk atop the stairs, two blankets each."

Lars gave a promising nod to Aaron, "An attic is as good as a room with a view. How much does the attic cost?"

"A simple coin that even a street-walker can afford."

"Well, we have not walked many streets but can afford your price," Aaron peered into her eyes. "Does the man, who we did offend, intend to return tonight; we would not want to be disturbed in our slumber. Times have been hard for me and my friend, and the last thing either of us would want is to be disturbed at an untimely hour."

"It is unlikely that he will return, but if he does my lips will remain sealed, and the one you refer to is Martin," advised the wench.

"A common name," said Aaron, thinking of his friend.

"For a common thief," added the wench. She turned to attend the weathered man and returned. "The attic can be reached via the staircase, over by the corner."

"Thank you, fair maiden, and take this, another coin for your lips of iron" The bar wench smiled at the stranger's generosity

"And do not disturb the rats; the last thing I need is to be disturbed by rodents shifting their nesting area from roof to floor. Oh, and one last measure of convenience for you two gentlemen." She reached under the counter and pulled a candle from beneath it. "Light this via the lantern above that table and be careful to extinguish the candle before you sleep. The last thing I need is a fire aloft."

Thirteen

Tu ne cede malis, sed contra audentior ito

The story or Raoul.

It was a long road, a road filled with danger. Raoul was a common soldier whose only dream was to be a knight, to serve those that were much like him in his days of youth, peasants through and through.

He was amongst a gathering of 2,000 men, women, and children, on a journey to Constantinople, to mingle with those within the triple walled fortress, to protect the crusaders against the Muslim hordes whilst on their long journey. But his task was more important than that of salvation alone. He was a protector; he was here to aid those that wished to travel the dangerous road to Constantinople. He was paid very little for what he did but money was not an issue for him. He would serve the emperor and the people for free if it was possible for him to do so.

The walk was long and hard, a journey of many weeks, time to think things through, to pin point ones place in life, to consider the realities of existence, and of God and His son, of all things religious, even time enough to consider the religion of his enemy, those of Islam and their slanderous ways, the torture, their belief, the death and slaughter which covered the land. Yes indeed, there was much time to contemplate many things in life, and life itself.

The Hospitaller Knights were scattered in units to the front, flank, and to the rear of those that travelled this way, a long line of helpless farmers, the deserted, the helpless, and the frail, young and old.

It was during the journey by foot that a knight of the Hospital came past his flank, upon a horse with a beautiful coat and mane. He slowed the horse down and rode with no effort at all alongside Raoul, looking down upon him from high upon his horse. Raoul looked back and then the knight dismounted, took the reins in his hand and walked beside him.

"My name is Anthony. What is yours?"

"I am known as Raoul."

"Raoul; I have seen you before," said the knight. "Where?"

"It could be almost anywhere, for there have been many times that I have come into direct contact with your Order whilst on escort duty such as this."

"You have protected before?" asked the knight.

"Yes, many times."

They looked at each other in contemplation as the walk continued, thousands around them paying no attention to the conversation taking place.

"Yes, I remember now," said the knight. "I have seen you many times, each time you walk with the peasants, you talk with them when resting, you help them cook their meals, and you play with their children as though one of them." There was a little silence then. "Why?"

"Why?" replied Raoul. "I love these people. Even if I was a knight like yourself I would still take the time to spend a little of the day with the common people. I am one with them. I would not volunteer my services to walk this dangerous trek more than once if I did not care."

"You volunteer?"

"I have changed units many times just to be able to protect the innocent," said Raoul. "So yes; although I receive payment, it is by way of my volunteering for this duty that I receive it.

"Why?"

"I have told you why, but more importantly you have seen why. You have seen me with your own eyes. What you see is what I am. I cannot help being in love with the people, to serve them as best I can. I would give my life for the children."

"You are romantic at heart," said the knight. "Such romance can be a killer."

"It would be my honour, so long as the innocent are saved from the curses of torture and rape so often inflicted upon them by those of Islam."

"You are one of a kind, Raoul. I shall remember you." And with that said the knight remounted his horse and rode off to the front, to see to his other duties.

A week had come to pass. The camp fires were burning and pickets had been placed. The knight, who had introduced himself as Anthony, came upon Raoul as he sat with the innocent around a fire, cooking their gruel and talking heartedly amongst themselves.

"Hello, Raoul," said the knight in greeting as he walked over to the seated form of the man that had intrigued him.

Raoul stood up immediately and stepped out of the circle of friends, "Ah, Anthony. A surprise it is to see you."

"I notice that you are taking some time to spend with the people," said the knight as they walked a little, away from the fire.

"It is my way. I cannot serve the Lord directly so I tend to his flock. It is my way of paying homage, yet I feel as though I can do much more. Do you know what it is like, Anthony, to be shackled to a bedpan of duty, to serve without restriction, but to love the serving? But I sometimes wish for more than the simple life of being a protector? Being a simple soldier is not my place but I do the best that I can."

"Yes, I know how you feel," said the knight with conviction as the flickering of the camp fires showed up within the pupils of his eyes; Raoul could see he was talking the truth and with much sincerity. "I, too, was much like you, before I became a knight."

"How did you become a knight?"

"I was chosen by a scout of the Hospital about twenty years ago and since then have become a scout myself."

"A scout? You scout forward of the march, scout the terrain

for the enemy in ambush?"

"Not that sort of a scout, Raoul," they stopped walking and turned to face each other. "I scout for the Order, to find men to recruit, worthy men that are known to serve with their heart and soul."

Raoul did not see what the knight was up to. "It must be a very hard job, yours. Trying to decipher such souls cannot be an easy task."

"Sometimes it is easier than you should think," said the knight. "Listen, Raoul. How would you like to meet a man, a man of the Order that could get you inducted, to have you issued with a black tunic, a tunic with a white cross?"

Raoul could not believe his ears but understood the meaning of the knight immediately. He was being recruited by the Hospital, to become a knight, to be a soldier of soldiers. "I can hardly believe what I am hearing. We have not spoken a single word since we last met."

"I have asked around, it is my job; and I have been watching. I know you now more than you know yourself," Anthony placed his open palms onto Raoul's shoulders. "You are to be recruited, Raoul, believe it, for it is true."

Fourteen

Tu ne cede malis, sed contra audentior ito

Martin and Raoul were much relieved by the hospitality of the convent. Although they did not get to see the mother superior that night, they were promised an audience the following day. The children were bedded down for the night in front of the huge fireplace and it was here that the two knights decided to remain, standing guard against the unlikely intrusion of any undesirables.

"Raoul, you take the first nap and I shall watch," said Martin, "for I am not that tired."

"It would seem that both of us are wide awake and with nothing to do," added Raoul. "It will be a long night, tonight, but the young ones deserve the comforts of a warm sleep. To remain awake for the duration of night is little to suffer compared to the importance of their safety. We must do all that we can to ensure that they not only survive, but remain together."

"Too true, Raoul," said Martin, and he continued, "I wonder how Stephen has done with his meeting with Father Ambaedian?"

"I should hope that it is successful, otherwise we will be in for a long search." Raoul searched his inner self then and let his thoughts be heard. "Do you trust in Stephen's dreams; I mean to say; can you believe he has the sight to see what is to come?"

"I do, and more still, he also sees the past, that which will be to our advantage."

"I heard him talking in his sleep one time, several weeks ago."

"Aye; and what did he say?" asked Martin.

"It was of a place far from here, across the sea, the same place that he spoke of during one of his many speeches, the land which we are to descend upon in all our glory. I know, it sounds absurd, the world we live in not being flat, but round... but that was what he said in his dream, the same thing that he said to us all when he disclosed to us the journey we were to make, of a long voyage to the west, to a land rich in fruits never heard of before, and unsurmountable gold."

Martin shot with a gleaming glare, "Gold you say? I do not recall Stephen having said anything about gold."

"It was the Templar's gold," added Raoul. "Listen to me, Martin. There was a story told to me, many years ago. It was at a time before I was a knight, and it was a story of twenty-four knights of the temple. They took to sea with many galleys filled with treasure. They sailed towards the west and were never heard of again. There, Martin, that is our destiny as decided by Stephen, where much gold is waiting to be found."

"And what, in heaven's name," said Martin, "are we to do with so much gold?"

"Use it to our advantage, I suppose," replied Raoul.

"There does nott seem much to me that can be done with so much gold, when so far away from civilisation."

"Besides, it's not for us to be wealthy, but to do the Lord's work." And Raoul looked at Martin in the light from the flickering fireplace. "Whatever Stephen is to uncover, that is what we are here to protect."

"I have sworn myself to that very duty."

"I have also sworn."

And both pondered the likely chance of their long voyage to the west. Much was still unclear to them and answers were needed for all of the men to feel the comfort so desired, for the mind was a fragile piece of organic matter. But all they had witnessed to date did instil great confidence within them, but time passed slowly and an end to the journey was desired by all.

Stephen told his story, of the chest and its power, of the verses carved upon it, and Ambaedian did not disappoint, he remained

alert for the entire hour, for the time that it took to tell the story, of the demise of Constantinople, and then Káros, of the thirteen orphans and their ill treatment in the hands of the devilish Turk.

"...and we are far from our journey, father," said Stephen. "We still have far to go, travelling west as far as the sea will allow us to travel. We must go where very few men have gone before. But having said that I must also reveal to you that many people do inhabit this land in which we are to settle, and they are at one with the land, living with it and not against."

Ambaedian sat beside Stephen and placed a palm upon his shoulder. The other two knights remained silent and listened to the pair sharing conversation.

"Stephen, I must tell you something of the Templar's past," said Father Ambaedian.

"Please, tell me all you can."

"I shall tell you a short story, one that will gel with your dreams, and you shall know the truth; listen to me, Stephen. At the time of the Templar's demise a group of twenty-four knights pooled together their resources. Each knight used his position of status well and organised for much treasure to be gathered at a small harbour called La Rochelle. This they did some months before the king of France began with his dismantling of the Templar's very society and being, torturing thousands and burning many more."

"I know the stories of their treatment, father. Such a heinous crime against the innocent that was. My dreams also concur with your story of the twenty-four knights."

"But it could not be stopped, the torture and mistreatment continued. So the knights got their treasure, hoarded from centuries past. They loaded the treasure onto eighteen galleys and set sail for the west. It was believed that the west would reveal to them something so grand that it did not seem possible, beyond their wildest dreams."

"I suffer a recurring dream, father, one where a man of gold stands before thousands, women of the same cloth, which too, I believe, is an army. He is known as the Golden Man."

"And do you know this man, Stephen?" questioned Ambaedian.

"Yes I do, for it is me."

The wretched soul of Martin, the man so bitterly undermined by Aaron and Lars did approach the sheriff's office. It was a normal dwelling and housed just one – and his wife. No bars to speak of, the sheriff's house was just that, the gaol some distance away, closer to the centre of town and not likely to be visited in the current weather. He banged heavily against the door.

"Damn you heathen. Stop that damn banging," yelled a voice from aloft. A window opened and a head appeared to be battered by the wind and a little rain. "Damn you; what is it at this hour that demands my attention?"

"Sheriff, I am Martin."

"Martin; do I know Martin? No I do not, so why are you banging against my door at this hour?"

"I must report an undesirable," stated Martin.

"An undesirable; and who is that; a Turk, a Jew perhaps?"

"No, sheriff," Martin placed his right hand to the wound upon his chest. "A man inflicted this injury upon me, with an arrow; held in his hand I tell you... he thrashed out to kill me."

"Damn," the head disappeared and the window was quickly secured. Murmurs could then be heard but not quite made out as the cursing sheriff got dressed and approached the door. It opened, "Let me see your wound."

Martin pulled the cloth back which covered the wound, his shirt blotched with blood and stained much fabric due to the rain. "My wound seems to have stopped bleeding but it is to my horror that such a man still roams these streets."

"Not there, man, not in the rain. Quick, you better come in out of the cold; it does neither of us any good. Get in here and show me, show me properly."

Martin moved into the hall and the door was quickly closed behind him. "Roams these streets? How am I supposed to find a man who 'roams-these-streets' at this hour," questioned the sheriff methodically, not really caring to step out into the night. The wind was more than refreshing.

Both men stood in the stone cold corridor, discussing the matter.

"You should be reporting this to the gaoler, we have one on duty."

"Sheriff, you remember me not?"

"Remember?" the sheriff looked closer, "Ah, the man so sorely beaten by those reckless youths?"

Martin was embarrassed but hid it well, "Indeed, sheriff; not much a man can do against a small crowd."

"Yes, well; so what of your wound, where was it given?"

"Attacked I was, in the 'Refuge'."

"That den of thieves?"

"You show me a den without thieves and I will show you an honest man."

"Well spoken," said the sheriff. "How were you attacked?"

"A man leapt from his seat and stabbed me with his quarrel."

"For what reason?"

"No reason... maybe I knocked him accidentally."

The blank look upon the sheriff's face indicated that he did not fully believe Martin's story, for it seemed quite absurd and unbelievable. "Look... would you care for a medicinal drop, Martin, and then we can get all of this sorted out?"

"Thank you sheriff, I would be honoured."

"Please, this way." The sheriff showed Martin into the front room of the small dwelling, a luxury paid for by the king, for a sheriff was housed quite comfortably, paid for via the taxes collected. The sheriff was a fat man, quite prone to eating well, and over drank on every possible occasion. "The fire has almost died but still gives off some warmth."

"More than can be expected outside," said Martin.

Both men sat in comfortable chairs and looked at the fireplace as the sheriff poured some wine for them both. "So tell me, what should be done with this man?"

"I want justice for the wound and justice for the defamation brought upon me."

"Ah, yes, defamation is a killer to someone with a reputation," said the sheriff, eyeing Martin cautiously.

"My reputation is as good as any other man's," said Martin in defence.

"Aye. Do you think he is still at the 'Refuge' or will he be sought elsewhere?"

"He will be drinking as we speak, quite comfortable in the fact that no action will be brought against him; even an idol threat will not dislodge him."

"Did you pose such an idol threat?"

"I simply advised that the sheriff would be informed."

The sheriff tipped his glass up and emptied the contents before placing it upon a small chair-side table. "It is time to move, Martin; time to get the scum off of our streets and behind bars. Maybe then, when all is done, I can get back to sleep in the comfort of my bed."

Aaron and Lars traversed the stairs to the attic, 12 rungs to a small veranda, doors to rooms standing along both left and right, and there, to the far right was the short climb to the attic door. Lars held his candle high so both could see.

"To find comfort in an attic will be hard," said Aaron. Lars simply looked and nodded. "But it is easier to sleep in an attic than to sleep with the blade of a sword against your throat," and the door was pushed open and both men stepped within, blankets held tight against their chests.

The roof was high and a few pigeons could be seen to fly off through a small hole in the roof near where it met with the side of the building. The hard wooden ceiling on which they stood was bare and there was not a comfort to be seen.

"Over there, look, some straw and what looks like sacking for a pillow. Our friend has used this attic before," Lars looked to Aaron and shook his head, running his extended fingers over his open palm, meaning to convey that he found security within the fact that others had slept here, meaning that such a common occurrence brought with it peace of mind, and fewer rats. "I agree, Lars; it is safe and we shall sleep a good wink before tomorrow." They both laid their blankets down.

The two men put down their arms, sword and crossbow, to ready themselves for slumber, for a good sleep was never received when sailing upon the sea.

They both made themselves comfortable upon the straw mattresses and blew out the candle that Lars had placed upon a wooden beam. It was then that the full moon could be seen to give off a little illumination, light seeping through gaps in the roof from above and where the roof met the side of the building, where gutters ran its length... the storm had suddenly stopped, almost as suddenly as it had started. Such a phenomenal occurrence the storm was that it could hardly be believed. Lars lay back as did Aaron, side by side and sharing in each other's warmth, pulling the blankets over themselves as best they could.

"Lars, do you feel that we should remain at guard tonight?" and looked upon the man beside him, receiving a nod in acceptance of the suggestion, one more night to add to the many in which they had maintained a picket. "I look forward to the day when guard duty will be a thing of the past, but wonder when that will be." He looked upon Lars one more time. "Sleep, Lars, and I shall remain afoot, so to speak, for my share of tonight's watch. Good night to you, my friend," and Lars simply smiled before closing his eyes.

Fifteen

Tu ne cede malis, sed contra audentior ito

The sheriff entered the house of squalor with Martin close on his heels. They approached the wench. She could see who had entered and gave a smile, undeterred.

"I see that Martin has scurried away to fetch his dog," said the woman behind the counter.

"Is that the way you greet the law?" said the sheriff as he approached. "Do I not deserve a better greeting than that expected to be bestowed upon a common dog?"

"Everyone knows my standing. I commit no wrong-doing and pay homage where required. You need me as much as I need a good man in my bed, to keep me warm on these long, lonely, and cold nights."

The sheriff cared little and shook the comment from his mind, "I seek a man."

"You seek two men," corrected the wench, "and I have them netted for you," said the wench. "Ah, I see by the look upon your face that you are pleased with what I have done for you."

A short-lived smile disappeared from the sheriff's face, the folds of fat forming creases here and there. "This is not the first time you have aided me, and yet I still do not know your name."

"It is Marian," said the wench with a wink. "A woman who, even in my years so bold, could curl your toes; if it was not for my husband."

"Years so bold," laughed the sheriff. "Is that what they call old age? Tell me," he changed the subject to parry further insult and jocularity. "Where are the men we seek? Are they where I assume?"

"Yes, sheriff, in the attic and without escape."

The sheriff turned with Martin on his tail, "Come," and to the wench, as he turned, he stopped and paid a further comment. "One of these days I shall reward you for your kind hospitality."

The wench smiled as the two made their way towards the attic, watching them purposely for the time it took them to approach the entrance to the attic, for them to hand out their justice, to the demise of the two men asleep, for others had fallen by way of her mischief.

Aaron shook Lars quietly, in the hope of rousing him at this, their time of need, the light of the moon still providing a little aid to sight.

"Lars," he whispered. "Men approach in stealth."

Lars stirred and opened his eyes, looking upon Aaron for further information. "I could hear the boards creaking below and then stifle slightly, and then footsteps towards the rooms. I heard whispers again as conversation started, and; and I believe they approach with a dire need to fall upon us as we sleep."

Lars was wide awake now, quietly as can be, picking up his crossbow and feeding it a quarrel.

"They have purpose and that purpose is not sleep."

Aaron pulled his sword from his sheath, and side by side, Lars and Aaron got to their knees and then onto their feet, just able to stand tall with the attic roof slanted above. Aaron made for a better grip upon the hilt of his sword and Lars placed the stock of the crossbow within the saddle of his shoulder, ready to fire and reload.

The approach of the two stopped and a final whisper could be heard along with the familiar sound of a sword being drawn from a metal sheath. Suddenly the door to the attic burst open and Martin, the first to enter - to try and save face in the company of the sheriff - brought the brunt of the taught crossbow that Lars held in his hands.

The quarrel was heading for its mark, but Martin had seen the men standing in wait and had immediately stepped to the side, the point of the arrow tearing a long tear into cloth and skin, the pain hardly felt, Martin's mind being overrun by the adrenalin and rush of seeing the man with crossbow to his front. Lars, in all his years, in the surety of his prowess and familiarity with weapons, had missed his target – it was too late to lock in another and his sword lay beside his blanket. Martin was bleeding from the open wound but carried forth with his purpose, having pushed his cowardice well aside.

The roof was too low for a sword to be fed a swinging chop, a slash of fury from above, and the sheriff, having entered the attic once before, simply thrust outwards as he stepped forward, his long sword, carried for such a purpose as this, reaching out and becoming a complete surprise to Aaron, whose gut bore the delivery of the sword as a scabbard of flesh, the skin of his abdomen sliding up the sides of the sword as his body encased the cold of the weapon, Aaron's facial expression delivering unto his attacker that knowing look: the look of death. The sheriff pulled the sword free and Martin, as surprisingly as could be, fell upon Lars like a great oak, and Lars in his numbered years gave under the stress of power brought upon him; both men fell, one upon the other, and Aaron fell as death gripped him in its cold embrace.

Lars was powerless to do anything but look out to his right, just able to see Aaron with the contortion of death written heavily upon his face; why did not he parry, why did not he fight, what made the man of steel slow to react?

And ashamed of his own effort, Lars gave up all resistance, for the fight was over.

Sixteen

Tu ne cede malis, sed contra audentior ito

The story of Bernard.

The soldier, Bernard, had taken some leave from his unit, the fierce fighting over the past month having taken its toll on his injuries. He needed a rest, time to soak his old wounds in oil, to tenderise the soreness, to heal the scars upon his upper torso, to relieve just a little of the pain that hammered him day and night. Always pain, the trait of a professional. You either die in battle or gain a few extra scars. It was one or the other.

He had travelled much of the night and the time for the sun to rise had arrived. It commenced to say good morning to the day, coming up in front of him on his short trek into the west, to a country town where he knew that he would be provided what he was searching for; release from the pain that he suffered. It was a journey that he had made many times in his life, seeking to relieve himself of his burden, to replenish his supplies of oil that was rubbed into his wounds. Without the oil he would be surrendered to rubbing his wounds with his fingertips, massaging his scars for hours on end. The oil was a special blend, a blend of substances that he did not know, for if he did then he would not have to travel the journey he was currently on the road to make.

He was a strong man, but not too strong, for the strongest men that he had known had come to trouble on the battlefield... too slow to move, too slow in their reflexes, too idol to make for cover when cover needed to be sought. He was intelligent and capable of operating on his own, travelling from town to town in any country by himself, able to speak five different languages and quickly learning another three, able to read and write, though not as well as a scholar of languages. He had been travelling this way for some hours and decided to take a rest beneath a tree, just to the side of the road, where he could partake of some jerky and water from the bag he carried on his hip. It was here, beneath the tree as he sat, that he first met the priest. From down the road, from the direction he was travelling, he saw an open carriage being pulled by two horses, running scared, their nostrils ablaze with mists of cold as each breath was exhaled after being delivered to the lungs. The driver of the carriage was bent forward, whipping the horses as best he could, trying heaven and earth to get that little extra effort out of them. A man sat beside him, dressed in a simple cloth like that of a monk, looking over his shoulder as the carriage continued towards him... they were being chased.

Bernard acted quickly and slunk behind the tree, and just in time. The right hand wheel of the carriage gave way under the stresses produced and collapsed, throwing the monk head over heels and into some nearby bushes; the driver was not so lucky, falling forward and beneath the other wheel where he was crushed by the forward motion of the carriage before it came to rest. One of the two horses got up from the road and started pulling to get free from the wreck without success and remained unsettled for some time.

Those chasing the carriage were upon it in seconds, three smaller men who drew their swords immediately on dismounting, walking hurriedly towards where the priest had been thrown into the bushes. The monk was sore and knocked about by the fall but had no broken bones to speak of. He got to his feet and clambered from the bushes at the same time that two of the men reached him and grabbed either arm. Not a word passed behind them, they acted as though acting upon an unwavering plot, and it was not until they had dragged him over to the upright wheel of the carriage still intact, that the first words spoken came from the third man as the other two tied the priest fast to the wheel.

"Where is it, where is the key?" the third man said, lashing out with a backhander across the priest's face. "The key, where is it?" Still no answer. "Search his pockets," commanded the man of the other two, as he turned and walked about in his impatience, pounding his fist into his palm, an evil grimace upon his face.

Both of the other men set upon throwing their fists into the pockets of the priest's clothing, fumbling around a little until one of them pulled out a wooden artefact. "I have it. Here it is; look."

"So plain it is, hard to believe that the Abbott wishes to pay so much for it," said the third, taking it from the other and looking at it closely, turning it over and over in his hand, trying heaven and earth to understand its mystique.

"Do not relinquish it to the Abbott," the priest cried. "For all our sakes it must remain with me."

"Shut up, you, we are going to fetch much gold for our part in this, so you just shut up," said the third. "The Abbott has paid a little for our services and has promised to pay a lot more on delivery. We will do as we have been bid, and once it has been delivered we will be very rich."

Bernard could see without much trouble that the priest was the innocent victim and that the other three meant to harm and rob the priest, but not only this, but they also failed to pay any attention to the man crushed by the wheel, for he might very well still be breathing. He could hear a few words being spoken by the third man as he paced up and down in front of the priest, but most of what he said could not be deciphered. He needed to make a decision, one that he knew was right.

He stepped from behind the tree. These three men before him would be no match for his skills in the handling of sword. He was not afraid to take them one, either one at a time or all in a single bout of fighting with weapons drawn.

"Excuse me gentlemen," said Bernard without as much as a heartbeat falling out of place. His nerve was steady and he did not flinch.

The three men turned together, startled by the intrusion, fear immediately gripping them, for they did not know who this man was or whether or not he had company. But the fear quickly dissipated and they all smiled, for they could see an easy fight before them, and when this man before them was dead then they would empty his pockets of whatever he carried.

"Who are you and what do you want?" asked one of the men with little concern for the answer, for no matter what Bernard said, there was going to be a fight.

"You should have been on your way, this is no concern of yours," said another, "but it is too late now."

"Oh, but it is my concern," said Bernard as he withdrew his sword from its sheath. "For I prey on cowardice, like you three prey on the innocent," and stepped closer to the group of three.

The three men brought their swords to the ready, held them out, perpendicular, ready to party with the single man in front of them, commencing slowly to encircle him. None of them took their eyes from him for a second.

"This is your first and last chance," said one. "Put down your weapon and we shall see to it that you are gagged and tied, but live you shall." The lie was transparent and seen for what it was.

"I am not a dog, so cannot run away or be allowed to wear a collar, so I guess I'll have to die..." said Bernard, "when my time has come."

"Your time in now, stranger," said the third, the leader of the pack.

The first of the three rushed in from behind, and Bernard quickly side-stepped and thrust his sword into the man's flank, withdrawing the sword again as blood rushed from the wound, the man falling to the ground in a heap. A second then used this as his opportunity to slash down with his sword from high above his head. The momentum of the sword swing could not be stopped and Bernard once again side-stepped out of the way employing a simple push of his sword into the stomach of his assailant. He too fell to the ground in a heap, clutching his open wound and started coughing blood.

"One on one," said Bernard. "Sounds fair to me."

The last of the three dropped his sword and turned tail to run, and to keep on running until he was far from danger. Bernard simply watched on for a while, sheathing his weapon, watching to ensure that he did not turn around and attempt to approach from the rear with a dagger drawn.

Bernard raced over to check on the fallen man beneath the wheel; he was dead; he then attended to where the priest was tied to the wheel and cut away the rope ties. He cut them quickly with his dagger and then put the dagger away.

"Thankyou stranger, thankyou for what you have done," said the priest as he looked around upon the ground, his eyes finally falling upon the key; it was safe. The thief had dropped the key on the road when confronted by the fight: it was so large and so very heavy; so much larger than any key he had seen before.

"It was my pleasure, I was happy to be of service," said Bernard as the last of the dying grimaces of pain departed the lips of the two men upon the ground. Two were dead and one had escaped, but the coward would not be back this day.

Bernard looked into the priest's eyes and introduced himself. "I am Bernard, plain and simple, no title."

"Thank you, Bernard," said the priest. "Please, let me introduce myself, I am Father Tourmede."

Stephen suddenly slumped heavily, back into the comfort of the chair, his shoulder slumping with the burden that fell upon him. The other two knights and Father Ambaedian could see that Stephen was horror struck, his eyes and face told how he felt.

"What is it, Stephen?" asked Ambaedian.

"Something; I am not sure," answered Stephen, and then with a suddenness that shocked his company he said, "Aaron is dead."

"That cannot be true," said Bernard.

"Certainly not," added Lambert.

And as though stinging with accusation, Stephen chastised the two knights. "How long have you known me? Do you still not believe, after all you have witnessed?" They understood their error and Stephen felt a wickedness never felt before, not just for the comment he had made against the two knights, but also for another death of a friend being delivered to them. "Please, forgive me." So much death had been witnessed, but now more than ever it hurt. Even where his wife of Constantinople was concerned he felt less pain, and why was that? It was the truth of the chest, it was Stephen's destiny which hung in the balance; he was to become immortal, but did not fully understand what that meant, did not know of the power which he was to possess.

"Forgiveness is not necessary," said Lambert.

"Certainly not where I am concerned," added Bernard.

And a few seconds of silent contemplation was disturbed by Father Ambaedian. "The time has come, Stephen." He stood from his chair. "We cannot wait any longer, the chest must be opened, and the two powers that we find within must be fused." And with the comment came stares of agreement, and Stephen nodded acceptance of the task that remained undone. They had ventured here for a reason and that was to fuse the good and the bad of the chest; and so it would be done.

"I agree," said Stephen, "we cannot delay it any longer."

Seventeen

Tu ne cede malis, sed contra audentior ito

Abu and Ahmad were lurking about when out of the shadows and along the cobbled way, so wet, came the footsteps and silhouettes of three figures. Abu and Ahmad took quickly to the shadows along the side of the buildings, pressing themselves out of sight, watching motionless as the three came to view.

"Move along, damn you," snarled the sheriff, pushing Lars from behind where his hands had been tied with thick rope. "Try to kill the sheriff and you try to kill the king."

"It was me he tried to kill, sheriff, not you," reminded Martin.

"He knew not who he fired against, that may be true, but I was his mark as much as you," was his sound reply, and then another push in the back for Lars did follow. "And why do you not talk, ah? You damn bastard. You shoot you quarrels to kill but fail to hit your target, and at such close range, and why, why try to kill us, ah? Answer me you bum-of-the-street!"

"He cannot talk, sheriff."

"What was that? What do you mean?"

And from the shadows, Abu and Ahmad followed in quiet servitude to their purpose.

"Did you not see? He has no tongue."

"What?" they both stopped in their tracks, the sheriff followed by Martin, turning Lars around, the sheriff's palms placed either side of Lars' head and pushing it back for the light of the moon to ally with his need. "Open up, you bastard!" and when the truth was revealed, the sheriff stammered. "Ah, it is true, no tongue, well I never did see..." and saddened by the reality, added, "Not much point in interrogation, is there."

"Maybe he is a learned man," said Martin.

"A what?"

"Maybe he knows how to read and write."

"Do you know how to read and write?" asked the sheriff of Martin.

He shook his head.

"No, I thought not, a man of your calibre; I know your sort. A dumb ox to be sure," said the sheriff and after a short degree of concentration, "It will be just as fair to see this man rot in the dungeons, or hung by the neck until dead."

Abu held out his hand, pushing Ahmad back into the shadows as he strained to hear. The last thing Abu wanted was for Lars to die, for the man was his only link to the chest of secret's: thus far; but if it were true, if Lars could not talk then it was a fine mess he was in.

"Straight to gaol for you my friend-with-no-tongue, and before this weekend is over I shall see swift justice. I shall see you hanged for your contempt of the law, and I shall invite the entire town to see what the law delivers," and so on they trod, several pushes in the back to accommodate a speedy delivery unto the gaoler and his cells.

Abu held his hand in place, restraining Ahmad from following.

"They are getting away, Abu."

"That is okay, Ahmad. We no longer need to follow."

"But he is our link to the chest," complained Ahmad. "If we lose him... we lose—"

"Nothing, Ahmad; we lose nothing." An explanation was called for. "He has no tongue, so cannot talk, but his hanging... that will bring his friends out-of-hiding, and when his friends have been revealed to us we shall see the chest delivered into our hand."

"But we do not know what any of them looks like, Abu."

"We shall know; by their own doing, we shall see who it is that has the chest, for they will be the only ones not cheering when the man is hanged."

 *Eighteen*

Tu ne cede malis, sed contra audentior ito

The two knights placed the chest in front of them and took their seats, all four men relaxed and waiting. Stephen looked to Ambaedian and he stared back, each waiting for a cue, for a prompt on which to act. After a minute....

"The time has come then," said Stephen, "to open the chest once more."

"And this shall be the last," said Ambaedian."

"The last, why is that?" asked Stephen. "And what does it mean 'to be fused'?" and although Father Tourmede had mentioned briefly about the fusing of good and evil, Stephen could not fully understand the need, what it meant, nor the real purpose: he only surmised.

"Within the chest, or so it is written, are several artefacts which have specific meaning," said Ambaedian, and seeing that he had the attention of all three went into a detailed explanation. "You all know how Jesus met with death, the horrors of it. Such a death was delivered to so many, thousands upon untold thousands. Even at the time of Spartacus over six thousand souls suffered at a single crucifixion. The untold horrors of dying on the cross were known well before the crucifixion of Christ. But Jesus was the son of God, so it is written. There was a single man who tempted God's anger, and God delivered the fury of his almighty power to earth that day when the soldier prodded at the body of Jesus. With a pilum he prodded, a six-foot spear shod at one end with a wicked looking eighteen inches of iron, tapered to a point. With this point he spilled what was of Jesus' sacred temple; his body spilled to the earth like common dregs from a forgotten cup. It is this point, the point of the pilum that dealt such a savage and unmolested blow, that is considered, at the time, of a most heinous piece of justice delivered, that can be found within the chest. I know this as though I see it." And Stephen somehow knew it to be true. "This is the first item to be found in the chest and it is this which is evil. It delivers to all that are impure, almost instantaneous death. As though strangled of life you will meet with your destiny," And this was the same as Stephen had told Father Ambaedian, of what had happened at the temple of Káros. "It resembles the temptation of man, the indisputable contempt to infuriate the pure, to denounce the sacred existence of all that is good. Impurity strengthens the devil as he does seek to be strengthened, to deny Christ and His father as he, the Devil, does worship impurity from the fiery pits of hell. The pilum draws together and binds all that is evil in an attempt to strangle all that is good. That is what it represents, that is the evil housed within the chest."

"So much evil," said Bernard.

"And what is good?" asked Lambert.

"You shall seek no further than the widow," answered Ambaedian. "For it is written: Jesus sat down opposite the place where the offerings were put and watched the crowd putting their money into the temple treasury. Many rich people threw in large amounts. But a poor widow came and put in two very small copper coins, which equals a quadrans coin. Calling his disciples to him, Jesus said, 'I tell you the truth, this poor widow has put more into the treasury than all the others. They all gave out of their wealth; but she, out of her poverty, put in everything, all she had to live on'." Ambaedian looked at each of the knights and Stephen, one at a time. "This is what is good and shall remain the sign of giving for all time. No other action alone can surmount to more than what the widow gave. So two coins can be found within the chest, two copper coins that resemble the good of humanity. These things are to be fused as one, the good fused with the bad, and with it comes salvation, and only one will suffer."

"For one to suffer?" asked Bernard.

"Only one person shall reap the horrors which are comparable to those that Christ suffered."

"To suffer such cruelty," said Bernard, "cannot be a gift, cannot be salvation. Why would we fuse the good with the bad?"

"Firstly," said Ambaedian. "So that the Christian Church cannot be toppled by the Muslim unfaithful, by their demise of the Christian Church, and even those that believe they are pure may house something evil within them, even if they know not what they hide."

"And secondly," interrupted Stephen, "one must suffer as Christ, but for eternity, by living for the remainder of time, never to die, never to rot, never to be allowed into the house of heaven."

"That cannot be," said Lambert looking to the others in turn. "Such suffering should not have to be for one to suffer; and who should it be," he asked. "Not you, father, not you, surely."

"No," said Stephen. "It is I that shall suffer."

Lars sat within his cell, dried blood upon his face. There was no window for which to see the stars, no window for which to allow the light of the moon to aid him in sight. There were no bars, just a cell door, and within the door a small rectangle, which, when opened, revealed a little light from the corridor on the other side, where other cells joined the dark surrounds of the gaoler's walk. He knew he was alone because he could clearly recall his being thrown into the cell, assisted by another punch into the back of his head, a measure of criminality to accompany his gaoling. It was then, as he was pushed so haphazardly into the confines of the empty cell that he tripped and banged his head upon the rear wall, which knocked him unconscious.

He patted himself slowly and could confirm where bruises were, where injury had been sustained. He had been beaten well, before being plunged into darkness, but no manner of beating was going to get him to talk: ha! He could not talk!

His fingers traced themselves around his swollen eyes, both

bloodied well by the punches of the gaoler, not the sheriff. The sheriff was too fond of watching the beating take place, not in delivering the blows himself. But he could recall one thing, the promise to have him hanged for his trouble. There was no defending himself amongst accusations for he could not speak, and all of those of the tavern in which he had partook would not say a word in his favour, for he was not a regular patron, despite his honesty.

From all perspectives Lars' situation did not look good and all he could do was contemplate the hanging to come, and of his poor friend Aaron, who had been unjustly killed by the hand of the law.

Suddenly, and without warning, the rectangle was opened and light from the outside spilled upon his face before being blotted out by the head of the gaoler, a thickset man with a large jaw and big nose. He rattled the keys upon his belt with his right hand, seemingly in effort to try and torment Lars, but there was no success on his part, for Lars could not be drawn from his thinking.

"You would like these keys, would you not, you murdering bastard," accused the gaoler without any knowledge for the reason that Lars was being punished. "I have heard the sheriff speak to others. The verdict has been reached and you shall be hanged on Sunday morning." Lars was shocked but in too much pain for the shock to show upon his face. "But you have been granted one favour this night, a meal and drink." The gaoler's face disappeared from view for the measliest of time and reappeared in its place was a bowl of gruel as it came tumbling in through the latched window and all over the cell floor. The gaoler laughed as he looked in, uncontrollably it would seem. "Lick it off the floor you scum, it is all you shall have this night; oh, and your drink." The gaoler grunted and untied the rope around his pants, loosening them sufficiently before urinating against the cell door where it met the floor. It was too dark to see but Lars could smell the urine as it seeped under the door. "And drink well." The small window was shut and laughter filled the corridor as the gaoler walked away to attend his other duties.

The Templar, two Hospitaller, and Father Ambaedian, had come to terms with what the chest was to reveal, but one other thing was missing from the cauldron of their minds. "One thing more is of importance to us all," said the father, peering at Stephen, knowing what Stephen did know: of his sacrifice. "It is within the book that I have upon my lap that something has been revealed to me." He patted the book as though a long-life companion. "Within it there are many secrets but one stands out amongst all others. It reveals that the evils of God's own work, the spirits of good and evil within the chest, can be controlled through one that has been chosen, and only the chosen one can carry the cross."

"The cross?" asked Lambert, for Stephen.

"Let me read from the book, which was written some time before the bible, when the thoughts of the works of Jesus were contemplated and far from being scribed." He turned to a marked page and commenced to read. "It reads: 'And God spoke to me, from over my shoulder, as the ink from my quill fluently spills over the pages of this book; containment can only be gained when one has been found, a knight so humble that his beginnings are his end, through lonesome passion of generations past does the knighted bear the burden of birth, for from such a knighted birth does no death come. He will know his way in life through verses and dreams where the reality of life and death become obscured through the meaning of life, and to that I mean the containment of the devil, the denying of unfaithful thought through action of mind and soul, to be pure in all his courage of action. Death will not come of him as it has my son, for my son gave up his life to pay for the sins of the many, so that they may be forgiven in worship as any mortal will forgive another, but so many impure exist within the multitudes that the chosen one must prevail the givings of the chest and come to reign over the earth as the protector of Jesus' sacrifice. The good and evil of my son's death shall be secreted to a chest, to lay in wait for the chosen one to open it; but be warned, death awaits the impure. The chest shall be of man size, easy to port, hard to enter, as specified in previous instruction, and the key, too, shall reveal its secret. The keys construction, in two halves, must be adhered to so that when the good and evil of the chest are fused the Cross of Christ will be born. The cross is the salvation of man where the chosen one maintains it. With it comes many qualities too valuable to be revealed within the text of my verses. The chosen one will become one with the cross and with it comes the purification of the world. Generations hence will be swallowed from existence before I shall make visit unto the earth, and only with my acceptance, that men and women of the world deserve my son's sacrifice, will death be granted the cross's bearer'."

Ambaedian closed the book. "The key to the chest is made from two halves, so meticulously put together that the flaw within it cannot be seen. To pull the key apart before the chest is opened could destroy the key and mankind's chance for salvation. The chest must be opened before the key can be forced into two halves, and before the good and evil doings of the chest can be fused." Father Ambaedian went into further explanation. "I have read much of God's words and have come to understand what must happen. The message is subtle and straight forward. Once the chest has been opened the contents must be fused, melted and moulded, casting a cross from within the mould of the key. The key will become useless and so will the chest; it must all be burnt and discarded into the sea so that no man or beast can find the remains. Once the Cross of Christ has been scored from the cast then it must be placed upon a chain and then around the neck of the chosen one. The chosen one must remain apart from civilisation, as best as is humanly possible, in order to protect the salvation of the human race. An order of knights will be formed, and only the chosen one will know how to go about such forming.

"The Cross of Christ must remain in the hands of the chosen one for all time. If the cross is separated from its holder then damnation will be inherited upon the earth." The silence was set, many thoughts flooded the minds of Lambert and Bernard, but Stephen, he somehow knew what was to come, dreams he had received, voices in his head, and he knew that a cast of women would be born unto the earth, a cast of women that would be the salvation of the human race, protectors of the key and its bearer, protectors of Jesus' very sacrifice; one sacrifice for another.

"Thank you, Father Ambaedian," said Stephen. "You have clarified for me what I have anticipated these past few weeks. The voices within my head have drained away but the dreams I have are coming thick and fast. There are so many dreams that I cannot depict between one and the other, they come tripping over one another and cannot be controlled."

"You will learn to control them, Stephen," said Father Ambaedian. "You have the remainder of existence to learn."

Stephen looked at the priest and said with much conviction, "And that time must commence immediately. Let us open the chest."

Ambaedian stood up and the others followed his action. "First we must get ready with the fire," and with that said, Father Ambaedian looked to Lambert. "You must leave this house and turn left, follow the road to the top of the hill. There are no houses at the top of the hill. Once at the top you will notice a small smithy station on the reverse slope. Go to the side door and knock five times. When the door is opened, tell the man or woman that opens it, Father 'Ambaedian is ready'. They will know what to do. You will be asked to enter. Do you understand?"

"Yes, father."

"Go now."

As Lambert departed the company, Ambaedian continued with instruction. "We shall wait here long enough for the fire to gain heat. Once it is hot enough, Lambert will be sent back. We will then attend the smithy station. The smithy and his wife will have vacated the premises in order for us to do as we need to do with the fusing of the good with the bad."

Bernard looked to the priest and asked, "How did you know"

"I have the book," said he in answer, "and like Stephen, I have dreams too."

A knocking came at the door and Father Ambaedian stood immediately. "It is Lambert, back from the smithy station." He directed the others accordingly. "Bernard, go and let him in, Stephen and I will get ready the chest." Bernard nodded and retreated to the door. "Are you ready Stephen? For this is the first day of the rest of your life."

"I have been ready for a long time, father," answered Stephen with such conviction that his words could not be doubted. The two of them lifted the chest onto a small table. "As soon as the other two knights are here we shall proceed," and soon after those words had been spoken, they entered the confines of the room, Lambert and Barnard ready by their side. "Ah, good. Let us proceed. Please, Stephen, produce the key and open the chest."

Stephen put his hand into his pocket and pulled it out, the prized possession, for all to see in their silence. He slowly approached the chest and placed the key into it. It turned effortlessly and with such smooth action that Stephen was quite surprised. The key was indeed, well crafted. He looked to the others in turn and stared one final time at the lid of the chest before lifting it and standing back. He looked around and saw the others smiling as the Holy Spirit did transcend from the chest and sped off through the very roof of the house, as though into heaven. And as the Holy Spirit disappeared from view a voice fell upon the few, the voice of the Holy Spirit was delivering to them a message as it did in Káros, again, the same sweet message to the ear, so sweet that it had to be heard to be understood. Alas, Stephen neither saw nor heard any of it, for he was the chosen one. And within the time it takes to consume several breaths of air the miracle was over, Lambert, Bernard, and Father Ambaedian, looking to one another with a smile before finally Ambaedian broke the silence.

"I would never have believed that such beauty existed."

"What was it like, father?" asked Stephen.

"Did you not see it?"

"No, I did not."

"Ah, Stephen, you have truly missed a miracle of miracles. The Holy Spirit was lifted from the chest and spoke to me." He looked to Lambert and Bernard. "Did the Holy Spirit speak to you, did it?"

"Yes, father," answered Lambert.

"Me too," said Bernard.

"So beautiful it was, like music to my ear; but you, Stephen, you have a miracle of your own to perform, and we must not waste any time in seeing it carried out." It was then that Stephen took a step forward and looked into the chest, and there he saw what was to be expected, three items; two coins and the point of a pilum, secured into a scored recess within the wood, but for the pilum, it was the point only, enough metal between the three items to mould a large cross. "I shall carry these items in my pocket, the key in the other. Lambert and Bernard, carry the chest, it must be purified in flame after the Cross of Christ has been born unto the world." The three men simply looked with a smile upon Stephen and smiled, before acting quickly to carry out his commands, for he was the knight of knights.

"Come quickly, all of you, follow me." Something had transcended over Stephen, like a magical vale. His tone was kind and forgiving, but strong in command and steadfast in virtue. He lead the way out of the door followed by the porters of the chest and Father Ambaedian, to the left and up the road, to the smithy station on the reverse slope where the fire awaited them, the smithy cauldron, the blazing flames that were to melt the pilum and coins into their newest form, to be fused as one, to be cast into a cross. Stephen knew where to go without thinking, as though he had been here before. Through the house he trod, through another door and into the work shed. The blazing fire was there with the instruments ready for action, an iron cup on the end of an iron shaft, ready for them to place the contents of Stephen's pocket into the cup. He did this quickly and the chest was brought in and placed down, the cup with the pilum and coins now placed over the fire of the cauldron, placed to rest upon the furnace where flames licked up and over the items of good and evil.

The silence was intense and all that could be heard was the fire as it crackled and cackled, voicing what seemed to be the verse of many in conversation. The heat from the fire was stable but radiated well and the two coins started to melt.

Father Ambaedian looked to Lambert and Bernard. "Search for an urn, something as large as a wash basin, but smaller than two, an empty chalice for which to place the ashes of the chest. It will take a long time for the chest to be turned into powder. It must be allowed to burn and char, turned into ashes amongst the red hot coals, and when the coals have burnt out, what is left shall be secured in the makeshift urn."

"I have it," said Lambert. "Here, a basin with a lid."

"To secure the contents," added Ambaedian. "To prevent spillage." He turned to Stephen. "How are the contents of the cup?"

Stephen held his arm across his face and looked into the cup as the pilum commenced to melt at its outer edges, where the blade was thinnest, white hot and started to give in to the heat of the fire. "I think the cup will melt before the pilum," he said.

Ambaedian knew he was not serious: "The pilum will melt as required; the iron is old and frail; give it a chance." Father Ambaedian turned on his heels and went to the side of the workshop, lifting an hourglass up for all to see. He turned it up-side-down and placed it back down. "When the sands have drained away, the task will well and truly have been completed; sit and rest."

Only a quarter of the sands from the upturned glass had passed from top to bottom. Father Ambaedian stood and stepped over the furnace of coal and cup. "Stephen, my eyes are frail, it's hot and bright; what do you see?"

Stephen stepped up and looked into the cup seeing molten iron bubbling away. "It appears to be ready." He looked to the key which rested in his palm. "We are ready to split the key...? But, father; will the key not melt or burn? And the cross, it will be sodden with pits and cracks, it might not even have time to cool sufficiently."

"Stephen, you are creating a cross as though spoken from God," was the priest's answer. "We are creating something unique, something which will, forever, resemble the saviour of mankind. It does not have to look pretty."

Stephen understood something then, something which flashed before him, something that he did not wish to reveal but felt he had little choice, for his understanding would reveal to the others the true meaning of what they were creating. "I was once told a story of a sacred chalice; it was called the Holy Grail. It was believed to be the most common of cups from which Jesus drank, not dotted with pearls, gems, or other stones of great worth, but an everyday, common cup. It was a dream story, something that held water but could not be proved, something that has passed along the grapevine, from story-teller to story-teller. I tell you now that the cup is false for I know the true meaning of the Grail of Christ. This cross, no matter how common it shall be, once it is made will be the envy of the world, but the world will not know of its existence. The cross we are about to create is the Holy Grail."

And they all understood the words of Stephen to be the truth, for he had the insight, he had the power to be legend.

Stephen passed the key to Ambaedian. "Quickly, father, split the key as I make ready with the molten contents."

Father Ambaedian took the key as Lambert and Bernard looked on, both bewildered, dumb struck, without word and completely begotten by what they were about to witness, for they believed every word that Stephen spoke, and why should they not, for he was the chosen one?

The priest handled the key magnificently and with the key held in his left hand he placed a chisel upon its end with his right. Transferring his grip so that his left hand held both items, he picked up a hammer with his right hand, and commenced to hit the chisel, softly at first, until the key split perfectly into two pieces.

There before them was the key in two halves, one piece hollowed out sufficiently to form both the front and the back of the cross. A design could be seen but not made out properly: not only was there insufficient time to worry about that but as Stephen had already mentioned, it mattered not what the end result looked like, so long as it was true.

The molten iron was poured into one half, where the level of iron came up to the rim. He then placed the top portion into place, its inner face also holding a chiselled design, hence allowing for a beautiful mold both front and back of the cross, once cooled. The two parts, now together, were placed within an iron vice.

"The task is complete," said Bernard. "Once it has cooled we shall file its edges, make it smooth."

"Not quite complete," said Father Ambaedian. "For we still have a little molten iron left in the cup."

Stephen needed no prodding, no time to think, and acted immediately. "There is only one Holy Grail, what remains is of little consequence. Empty the cup of molten contents into a small tumbler of water. It shall be buried with the coals within a watery tomb, and if it should ever be found, which is highly unlikely, no one will ever scrutinize it, for it will have no appeal or lustre. Only one other thing remains to be done, one thing as important as important as the cross itself. We now must take it across the sea, into the west, where land can be secured and moulded to meet our needs, for the world is not flat, but round."

The four men looked at one another, nodding agreement.

The task was complete and the workshop had been cleaned up.

"What we have done here today shall remain a secret for all time. Never can the truth be spoken without permission first coming from me," spoke Stephen. "For the Holy Grail shall forever be bound around my neck and the contents of this basin, this makeshift urn, delivered unto the sea."

And as the four men, with the basin carried by Bernard alone, departed the workshop, a creaking grew from the hinges of a door. The smithy and his wife entered the workshop in astonishment to what they had seen through the crack of the door. In silence they had waited, had watched the cross being made, had heard the entire story develop as it had. They now understood why Father Ambaedian required being alone.

"My dear wife," said the smithy. "I think we have just witnessed something which could bring us much salvation."

"But how?" asked the wife.

"It must be worth something, to someone."

Stephen, Lambert, Bernard and Father Ambaedian soon found themselves in the comfort of the hall and its huge open fireplace, reflection of light from the fire flickering across the stone floor in orange hues.

Each sat down in silence before Father Ambaedian made the announcement. "I have something for you Stephen, something that you will carry with you for eternity... or I should hope so. I would like to think that a part of me will remain with you during your long and harsh journey."

"Whatever can it be, father?"

"Just you remain here in front of the fire and I shall be back shortly."

The priest stood up and made for the stairwell in the hallway and returned a short time after. He sat back down and learned forward from his seated posture, his right hand holding something. He held it out, "For you," he said and dropped into Stephen's open palm a simple chain of silver.

"It has been in this house for as long as I. When I started to read the many volumes I had collected over the years, which in itself was no easy feat, I came to the conclusion that the time would come when a chain would be required. I spoke with only a few trusted souls in regards to the chest and its secret, men of the Hospital all. The word went out to these few high priests, which is how you came to hear of me and decided to seek me out. A great chance I was taking for if the word had gotten out then I could have been in danger. Lucky for me that I never told the high priests any more than I had to. Of course, it was to come by way of word-by-mouth that a key was held in Káros. Once I heard this I set about revealing my information to Father Tourmede. He was a great man and knew what was good for the country and religion. So, at that time in my life, where I had studied all that I could from the volumes in my library, all I could do was set up house for the unfortunate and await the miracle to come. You, Stephen, are that miracle." There was a short break in the story before Father Ambaedian concluded with the obvious. "Use the chain for the Holy Grail, Stephen. Place it around your neck and never take it off."

Stephen put his hand into his pocket and drew out the cross, a design of magnificent structure raised upon the cross in the shape of Jesus, and the only impurities within the cross were a few, fine fissures that had appeared during its being moulded into shape; but it was strong, 3 x 5.5 pouce in size. The top most portion of the cross had a hole in it and through this he placed the chain, and the chain he put around his neck. It was not a ceremony worth noting, or by any degree requiring special service, but the silence in the hall that minute was only interrupted by the crackling of the fireplace as it continued to give off its radiant heat.

"This chain and the Holy Grail that it carries will forever remain a part of me," said Stephen. "Under no circumstances shall it be removed." And he tucked it back in behind the folds of cloth around his neck.

"That, young knight," said Ambaedian, "is not something you can afford to do."

 # *Nineteen*

Tu ne cede malis, sed contra audentior ito

Sister Bardwell approached the congregation of girls and their escort of two men as they had breakfast. The dining area catered well for large crowds, although no one else was present.

"Ah, Sister Bardwell," announced Martin as he stood, a smile appearing upon his face. "We must thank you again for these platters of bacon and mushroom. I can see that such morsels would not be easily afforded."

"Please, sit down," was the gentle reply, a little embarrassment felt, although such embarrassment did not show. "We have several members of the community who give quite often... not money, of course, but items such as pigs, goats, and wine. We also have an extensive garden."

"A garden?" asked Martin.

"One that takes much of our time, I am afraid, but well worth the effort, many vegetables being procured during the year. Many hungry mouths are content by our generosity, as we are content with the generosity of those that supply the means to procure a plate full of meat, cheese, or cup of milk. We are very grateful to all those that provide for us, in particular at hard times such as these, and it is seldom easy."

Martin saw an opening then and as all eyes looked upon him he offered the services of all of those that were eating. "I know the children would be more than happy to tend your garden, for your generosity at this, our time of need, is much appreciated."

"You flatter the convent with your words, Mr...."

"Please, call me Martin, I shall not allow us to be looked upon in a manner that is not deserved. Your work here, by-far, is more deserving than anything we could do."

Sister Bardwell catered for Martin's offer and took the opportunity for further conversation. "In that case, Martin, I shall have one of the other nuns tend to your flock by introducing them to our garden, and ask you to join me and the Mother Superior for further orientation."

The knight could see something was of the matter and nodded acceptance, "Tell the Mother Superior that Raoul and I look forward to the meeting." And with that said the nun departed company, leaving the group of children and two men to finish their morning meal in peace.

The children had been surrendered to work under one of the other nuns of the convent, picking weeds, tickling the ground with hoe and rake, although watering the vegetables as they grew was not required this day due to the storm the day before: along with any small task that was not too much for a young child to partake of, as Martin and Raoul sat in front of the warm fire of the main hall. They had not been waiting long before the Mother Superior entered the room with Sister Bardwell close on her heels.

"I see from the description given that you must be Martin, and you are obviously, Raoul?" said the Mother Superior, placing her hand out, which was accepted by both men with a smile. Such informality and ease made both men feel relaxed. "Please, sit back down; I would like to have a word with you both."

"Of course," said Martin and both men sat, followed immediately by the company that had entered.

"I shall get straight to the point, Martin, as it is not our way in life to waste what time we have, and I am sure, at most, that your time is as important to you as ours is to us."

"Of course, we both understand," replied Martin with a concerned look falling upon his face for the first time.

"It concerns the children, really. I need to know what your intentions are in regards to the children."

"We would like to leave them here for a few days and return

to collect them for a further journey."

"Sister Bardwell has told me as much," said the Mother Superior, suspicious of their real calling. "She advises that you have come all the way from Constantinople, and that the city has fallen?"

"That is correct; it now grieves under Muslim control."

"That is tragic news, but more tragic is the future of these children that you keep. Tell me, Martin, tell me of this school that you referred to last night, and tell me of your master and his overall plans for the children."

Raoul and Martin could both see the calamity of their situation most clearly. It was clear that the Mother Superior was concerned deeply for the welfare of the children, but nowhere near as concerned as they.

She broke the silence, "The children must have suffered much, as their clothing and appetite have suggested. Your voyage has been long and should have ended long ago, long before you came to Barcelona. It seems strange that you should travel so far, from Constantinople to here, to surrender the children to a school of which you seem to know nothing, a school which your 'master'," which she emphasized, "needs to lay visit upon before actually allowing the children to visit."

"Forgive us, but the rain last night was unforgiving. We could not allow the children to be harmed any more than was necessary. We simply require somewhere for the children to stay for a few days," Martin trailed off before making an offer. "We can pay for your trouble, for the charity which we require."

"Charity is charity, little or much, it remains the same. Payment is not required, as what we do is for the children. But let me ask you two gentlemen," and it appeared to Raoul and Martin both that the situation of turning-for-the-worst was beginning to show. "What business do you need to attend so urgently that you need to leave the children here?"

There was no answer to the question for the knights simply needed to have the children cared for whilst the situation with the Muslims could be taken care of. Raoul could see that Martin was slow to react to the question and he took the opportunity to answer for him.

"We need to shop for a wagon, some good horses to pull it, and rations enough to last the children a few days during our short journey," said Raoul.

"Ah, you have a voice," was the mother's superior answer of ridicule. "Tell me, Raoul, where is the school and what are your intentions once the children have been delivered? Are they to be left in the company of others, schooled until they are ready to fend for themselves? If this is the case then you might find comfort in knowing that you can leave them here at no further expense to yourselves, or your master."

"You are kind, Mother Superior, but our master has been very clear—"

"Then what is the name of the school you are referring to?" interrupted the Mother.

"We do not know the name," answered Martin.

"You travel all the way from Constantinople, with the pure intention of putting these children to school, yet you know not of the school's name," said the Mother Superior, making a statement, not posing a question. "It is also clear to me that your journey will take more than a few days for the only school and orphanages are those around Barcelona, and anything more would be a week's journey at least."

"Please, we are not criminals; you can see that our intentions are noble by the way the children look to us in their infectious way. We feel nothing less than the greatest concern for the children. We must wait for our master to return and continue with our journey. The children are our responsibility and must remain so."

"Very well, Martin," said the mother superior. "We shall give you and your master seven days. If in that time you have not returned to collect them, and with the name of the school that you are referring to, I shall take matters into my own hands and see to it that the children are placed into our custody. Do I make myself clear?"

"You do, and I thank you for your understanding," said Martin. "Could I please speak with the girl named Catherine before we part? We have much to do and need to pass on our goodbyes before we depart."

"Of course.

It was clear to Martin that their main plan of action was somewhat interrupted by the suspicious mind of the Mother Superior; he should have remained calm and in control, simply advising the Mother that Stephen was to meet them at the convent in a few days, but he had concerns for the situation in regards to the Muslims that had followed them. He was aware that Lars and Aaron were to tend the problem with the Muslims, and ensure that the enemy remained unaware as to their position, but he needed to make sure, even if to console himself. So long as the children remained in safe hands he would be able to scout around, it was even possible for him to gain important information that might be of use to them as a group. There was also the call to duty in regards to their second priority, to ensure that the carrack was ready for a retreat from the harbour of Barcelona: far from it for them to know that she had sunk.

Martin knelt beside Catherine with a smile as she continued with tending the garden. "Listen to me, child, and listen carefully. Raoul and I must attend to our urgent need, but we shall return. Tomorrow morning, as the sun breaks the horizon, you must have all of the children ready at the front door of this convent. You must be quiet and slip away during breakfast, not bringing attention to any of the Sisters that reside here. We will have Stephen with us." They locked eyes. "Do you understand, child? It must be a clean break."

"Yes, Martin," answered Catherine. "I understand."

Twenty

Tu ne cede malis, sed contra audentior ito

Stephen had a late rise, as did the others, but they were soon congregated in a private room where breakfast had been laid out for them all. The busy service of the home for sailors could be heard from where they sat, the platter of plates, the mingled conversation, laughter in places going uninterrupted. Father Ambaedian then entered as the three knights sat eating, reflecting individually on the previous night's activities.

The priest sat with all eyes upon him. "I have decided to join you, Stephen, back to the harbour where your carrack awaits. I am sure that you could use an extra hand to help you with your expedient departure. I also know some of the locals."

"Your help will be much appreciated, father," said Stephen. "I thank you from the bottom of my heart and..." suddenly, and without warning, Stephen clutched at the cross beneath his tunic and gasped a final heavy breath which he exhaled as though in disbelief.

The knights either side grabbed out at him to lend support where support might be needed. "It is okay, thank you Lambert; Bernard; I am okay now, but bad news I have witnessed. I only hope that the news I bear witness to is incorrect... I do not even know when... the cross is hard to decipher."

"With practise you will see all," encouraged Ambaedian. "But tell us, please. What did you see?"

"We must depart immediately for our friend Lars has been place into gaol."

"Gaoled?" asked Lambert

"I cannot see all and I do not know the reasons for his being arrested, but I see the hangman's noose being placed around his neck. I, too, can see the neck snap. The Lord will deliver to him a quick and painless death."

"There must be something that we can do," said Bernard. "We can rescue him, with the help of the Cross of Christ."

Stephen abruptly turned upon his friend, and Father Ambaedian also gave a horrified look, both of which fell upon Bernard's watchful eye.

"The cross can never be used for personal gain," said Stephen. "And never will I try. It is for the good of the human race, for the Christian religion, for all of those of Orthodox belief; it is even for those of Islam so that they may see the errors of their ways, so that the world can be joined as one. It cannot be used to relieve Lars of the justice that has to befall him. God has already granted him a pain-free death, that in itself is enough, and for that we should be forever thankful. But furthermore there is, I can see it now. Lars did cause action upon another which was an act of self-defence, but even so he must meet his end. Those that have caused this ill fate will be dealt with by the hand of God and Lars will live for eternity in the house of heaven. Lars has done more for us than he can be thanked for."

"He deserves your presence," said Ambaedian.

"I shall lay visit upon him and pass on the secret that we have unmasked. He shall be told all so that he can die in peace. A special prayer we will say for him when death takes him from us."

"I shall prepare a horse and cart immediately," advised Father Ambaedian, and although he did not know Lars, he did know one thing: if the knight known as Lars could be trusted by Stephen then he was worth every ounce of effort in allowing him a peaceful death.

"Thank you, father," said Stephen as he stood. "Lambert, Bernard, get ready the makeshift urn and its contents, we return to the harbour post-haste."

The cart made its way with a stinging of the whip behind the horses head, a jolting start to a reasonably short journey. What had taken the knights several hours to walk would now be considerably shorter. The weather was also good but the road was a little muddy, clouds had dissipated considerably, and birds had come out to greet the new day of bright light and warmth.

"We will be in the city of Barcelona before a hungry man has time to get a good fill of bread and wine," said Father Ambaedian. "It will not take us long."

Stephen sat beside the priest with Lambert and Bernard sitting opposite each other in the back, the basin placed securely upon the floor of the cart and between several dozen large bags filled with fruit and vegetables, commodities that the priest wished to sell whilst in the town they were to lay visit upon. Stephen looked at Martin.

"Martin, please pass me some fruit and a couple of pieces of vegetable," and once these had been handed over, Stephen placed it into his pocket. "Thank you, Martin." Stephen turned to the priest.

"I must thank you again, father. Your time in our errand is much appreciated," said Stephen.

"I shall not hear of it, Stephen. You have far too much to concern yourself with, and besides, I must get these vegetables to market, for the men who stay with me could do with a belly full of wine. It does not do well for the mortal man of town to go without a little vegetable."

"And for those of us who are no longer mortal?"

"You have a burden to carry, that is for sure, but I doubt for a single minute that you would be denied your rights as a man. Surely you will desire a woman from time to time, that is most natural. It is not as though you are ordained."

"I believe the contrary, father. I believe the Cross of Christ is an ordination, and I shall live as any other man of the cloth. Besides, I was married once."

"Really," said the priest, seemingly shocked. "So young in life and married. Where is your wife if not by your side?"

"She rests in the same place that the basin is to be delivered," said Stephen, and seeing Ambaedian's blank look gave further information. "She was surrendered unto the sea. She died in Constantinople and I was lucky to get her away. She was buried that same unfortunate day that Constantinople was taken by the heathen Turk."

"Such a young life lost," said the priest. "It must have been very painful for you."

"Yes, it was," agreed Stephen.

"How long were you married for?"

"Two and a half days, father," and Stephen could feel the shock of the priest without even looking. "We were wed on the Saturday night and Constantinople fell on the Tuesday morning. I have since vowed never to remarry." Stephen fondled the ring upon his finger, a ring that the priest had not come to notice until now. "I consider myself still married to her and could never marry another. If I am to believe that I am the chosen one, and that there is indeed life-after death, then I must assume, for all sakes, that I shall meet my wife again." Stephen looked to Father Ambaedian then, who met his stare briefly as he controlled the single horse carriage along its way. "I do not believe that my life will be eternal, but even if it is, I still have a wife. I cannot neglect her; even if I cannot see or touch her, it does not mean that she does not exist."

"I am going to help you, Stephen, as best I can," said Father Ambaedian. "We shall ride into Barcelona and lay visit upon your friend so that you may pass on your final words and prayer. Your other friends should not be hard to find. Where are you to meet them?"

"On the road that leads to the north, I can show you when we arrive in town."

"What are we to do once in town?" asked Lambert. "And when do we lay visit upon Lars?"

"You and Bernard can tend to the horse and cart, and the basin. I alone shall visit Lars. I shall meet up with you again later in the afternoon, and if luck is with us, both Martin and Raoul will have found us."

"And of Aaron?"

"We will not have time to attend any funeral. It is upsetting, I know," said Stephen. "To think that our friend will be delivered unto God's care in a common garden box, most definitely without the appropriate psalms to give appropriate praise to the honourable man he is. Much courage he did display."

Silence then dominated the scene as they continued on their way to Barcelona, reflection upon their friend Aaron. None knew of his past, at a time before he became a knight, but his time on Káros proved that he deserved to walk with all the brave men of the earth, in heaven. His courage was exemplary as too was his character and concerns for others. He never shirked a job and was always there to provide a helping hand. He would be sorely missed.

The smithy and his wife sat beside one another and followed those in front of them, making sure they maintained a very reasonable distance behind Father Ambaedian's horse and cart. Many thoughts crossed their minds as they continued with their slow pursuit, a journey into the unknown. For them the glory of life was not to be found in heaven, but was in their lust for gold and wealth. They wanted nothing more than to put their miserable life behind them so that they could lead one of luxury and ease.

"Do not get too close, my husband," said Patricia, his wife. "Ambaedian will recognize us if he sees us."

"Do you take me for a fool?" said Henry in reply. "I shall maintain good distance whilst on these country roads, but once we commence to enter town we shall have to gain ground on our friends; I would not wish to lose them in the crowd."

"What do you think of the Cross of Christ?" asked Patricia.

"What! Oh, the Holy Grail. It will be worth a hundred times its weight in gold... a thousand." He looked his wife of 25 years in the eye. "We are rich; I can feel the gold between my fingers already. We will have so much gold that we can shower ourselves in luxuries only dreamt of, and every day, too. I can see the wealth of it now. Servants we shall have, ten, twenty; and a butler and cook; a large house with a horse drawn carriage with driver and footman."

"Such wealth," said his wife. "But if the Holy Grail is all it is supposed to be... how do we get rich from such a thing?"

"We shall learn, like any other person learns a thing, we shall learn the trade of the grail. It will become second nature. And we will live for ever and a day, showered in its riches, like rain drops falling from the sky. Imagine it, just imagine."

And they continued on in silence, watching the cart in front of them as it made its way towards Barcelona. Their future was just out of reach and they both badly wanted it in their grasp.

Twenty-One

Tu ne cede malis, sed contra audentior ito

Martin and Raoul approached the harbour as inconspicuously as one could approach, the fresh morning breeze smelling of the sea, gutted fish and sweat. Sea gulls filled the air as they swarmed around, looking for morsels, for the guts of fish, their heads and fins, anything that the fisherman wished to give up to the squawking birds as they came down to the pier, hobbling around, resting on rail and rope, mast and bollard. The harbour was flush with activity, the boats being unloaded of their catch-of-the-day, filling the orders as they came from fishmongers.

Martin pointed off into the distance, towards the end of the pier.

"Just there, Raoul," said Martin. "That is where the carrack should be."

"I am bothered by the lack of what I see before me," said Raoul. "Do you recall what Stephen said to the master of the harbour when he was confronted by the man?"

"Yes, that the brigantine would pay... ah, there would have been none; no payment would have been received."

"And Stephen advised the master of the harbour to keep the carrack if no payment was forthcoming. Do you think he has moved it?"

"It would have proved to be too much to move by himself, and more than likely that moving it would have been a waste of time. What better position than where the carrack sat, for advertising a boat for sale. Any merchant would have been more than happy with the condition of the vessel. I have no doubt in my mind, Raoul, that the carrack would have been sold that same day that we entered harbour."

"No, it was too late, too dark, and too stormy."

"I see no other explanation."

"Maybe we should ask the man ourselves," suggested Raoul.

"I think not. It is more than likely that he will try and charge us for the time it was tied up."

"But if he sold it... we would be due compensation."

"You forget, Raoul. Stephen did give it away, more or less."

"So what now? What shall we do?"

"We shall attend the suggested meeting place as provided by Stephen. We will meet him there and advise him of the situation. There is nothing else we can do."

"Then let us move, and let us hope that he arrives today, for tomorrow we will have our hands full with tending to thirteen children."

Within the half hour, Martina and Raoul could see a horse and cart approaching from the north end of the road.

"Do you think that is Stephen?" asked Raoul.

"I cannot tell from this distance. Let us wait here in the shadows until it gets closer." So they pulled themselves back from the road and waited as the cart drew closer and closer. All they could see were two men, one sitting next to the other, reins gingerly held in the palm of the driver's hands, the horse moving along slowly with his head hung low, familiar with his surroundings and the road to Barcelona. Stephen was looking ahead and saw the meeting place to his front.

"That is it, father. That is where we must meet the others," said Stephen as he pointed off to where the road began, where a cobbled way melded into a dirt track, where the last of the town houses lined the street. "And there... can it be?"

Martin smiled, "It is Stephen, it is he," and pulled on Raoul's sleeve. They both moved out of the little shadow in which they stood and gave a short wave, Stephen holding his hand up for both men to see.

"Lambert, Bernard, we are there, I see Martin and Raoul standing on the side of the road, just to our front."

109

"Thank heavens they are safe," said Martin.

In no time at all the horse and cart pulled up beside the two men. "Climb aboard," said Stephen. "We shall find a place to stop the cart and continue with our tasks."

"Much to our disappointment," said Martin, "we have to part upon you bad news."

"We have much to discuss," said Stephen. "But it shall have to wait. Father, can you find somewhere to put this horse and cart of yours, somewhere out of the way?"

"I know a place, an alley beside a family-owned restaurant. They have been kind to me in the past and will not mind it if we leave it there. They will know my cart if they see it and it will be safe from prying eyes."

Martin and Raoul clambered aboard, sitting themselves beside their comrades of the Hospital.

"Bad news, Martin," said Lambert. "We have news that Aaron has been killed and that Lars has been imprisoned."

"Oh my god," exclaimed Martin. "How do you know for sure? Where is Lars now?"

"It is the secret of the chest," said Raoul. "Stephen has much to pass on, much to tell. The Cross of Christ has been born, but more than that, it is a secret that we have uncovered, something so wonderful that I still cannot believe it, but it is true."

"Please tell us," said Martin.

Stephen turned upon his seat and looked upon the men in the back of the cart. "Soon enough, Martin. You and Raoul will know everything, but for the meantime we must depart the comfort of the cart and prepare ourselves as best we can to the changing predicament."

"How was Aaron killed?" asked Martin, anxious for some news, unable to wait.

"I do not know exactly," said Stephen in reply. "But I do know this much; it was a cowardly act that had no real cause. They were both unjustly treated and condemned without sufficient proof."

The horse and cart had been left in the alley without a hitch and Stephen took the opportunity to familiarize himself with the bad news of Martin and Raoul. Stephen was turned side on, as was Father Ambaedian, to share conversation with the four knights in the back of the cart, the basin between them all, secured in place by heavy sacks of vegetables.

Stephen broke the silence and started the briefing. He explained in detail the opening of the chest and of what they had found within it, of the task they had in melting the objects and the secret of the key. The chest of secrets was no real mystery, in the end. It was the key, the key itself held the secret of the chest. From the key a cross had been created. The knights knew since they had left Káros that the contents of the chest had to be fused, but how it was to be undertaken had been a mystery of its own. But now, as Stephen explained it to them, it seemed to be nothing less than common sense. It all fit together: Káros, the key, and the chest.

"And furthermore, the Cross of Christ is nothing less than the Holy Grail," said Stephen.

"How can that be?" asked Raoul.

"It is a gift from God, a gift to set mankind free. Only the chosen one can hold the power of the grail and I am that chosen one."

"What are you to do, Stephen? What is your quest?" asked Martin.

"There is so much to tell that I do not know where to start, so please, bear with me," said Stephen, and he explained as best he could of the history of man and the task he had been set. It was for the chosen one to inherit the power of the Cross of Christ, also known as the Holy Grail; what is one, is the other. The power of the cross will be for the chosen one to decipher, to release, to hold, and to deliver. It is for him, the chosen one to be the protector of Jesus' sacrifice, as He did sacrifice his human existence so that the multitudes could be forgiven their sins. And why should anyone be forgiven their sins? Because it is not the fault of the sinful, but the fault of the devil himself, for the devil resides in the heart and minds of all, but it is for the individual to deny the devil. This is the meaning of life and will be the task of all men and women, for the remainder of all time to come, to take control and denounce the devil, at each and every opportunity. The chosen one must inherit his sacrifice with pride and good judgement, which is why he is the chosen one, chosen by the hand of God. For the chosen one's work to be completed to the best of his ability he must remain far away from civilization, for if the Cross of Christ was to fall into the wrong hands then damnation could easily befall the human race. Only the chosen one can behold the grail, the great artefact that was moulded from the good and evil of man's past. It was for the chosen one to protect the human race and to bring it salvation, but no good comes easily and many years must pass before salvation can be heralded amongst all religions, for they do not understand one another as God understands them all. The chosen one is to form an order of knights, the female of the species to be anointed by great responsibilities, and history has shown that only the female has the power of birth and man has the power of to deliver death; but the roles would be reversed: the female would become the hunter and the male of the species nothing more than a concubine, although only one man would ever couple with a single woman and a ceremony of marital worth staged for the sake of religious endeavour; the man and woman would not live together. The Holy Grail was of God's work, but the religious framework of the future would be that of Jesus and his New Testament. The Cross of Christ must be protected for the remainder of human history to come until such a time that salvation has been secured in the hearts and minds of all on earth. Only when everyone can clearly understand the sacrifices that Jesus bestowed upon us all can we truly be forgiven the sins of the devil and be considered as one. It was the orphans, the thirteen girls currently housed in the orphanage, that were the key to success in Stephen's mission. It was the girls that were the framework for the Knights of the Holy Grail. The girls would grow to become women, to harbour a name that would one day be whispered upon the lips of the entire world,

Coniupuyana, which means Amazon. These thirteen would be the women of the Amazon, a race of women so feared that they would become legendary. In order to secure the salvation of the human race the chosen one must travel west, for the earth was round, not flat, and he was to find the path to the treasures of the Templar Knight. It is written in history that 24 Knights of the Temple travelled amongst eighteen galleys, all filled to the brim with treasure, and such treasure was somewhere to be found, somewhere that only Stephen knew. Yes indeed, for they had departed from La Rochelle and were delivered unscathed upon the mouth of the Amazon. Stephen would find the treasure, hidden as it was. He would become known as the Golden man to some, the Gilded Man to others, and yet El Dorado to most. A legend would be born. It would be for the chosen one to suffer in his immortal existence, as Jesus suffered upon the cross, but with such a sacrifice came the power that God wished to relinquish, for Stephen would have unlimited power on life and death, would see the future and read men's thoughts. He would know what to do as though born to it.

"And that is the story as I know it, the truth, the whole truth, and nothing but the truth," concluded Stephen. "And now we have other matters to attend to. We must attend the carrack."

"The carrack is missing," said Raoul. "We attended the harbour this morning and could not find it. It has vanished. We decided against going to the harbour master for fear of being persecuted."

"You made a wise decision," said Stephen. "Father Ambaedian, can you help with securing another boat, one suitable for a small crew and thirteen passengers?"

"I think I can be of assistance, although the law may be broken in the process."

"The owners will be rewarded," said Stephen. "The power of the cross will see to that. I shall attend the prison where Lars has been wrongfully detained. Please take the four knights with you and do as you need to do."

"Where shall we meet?" asked the priest.

"I shall see you before last light, at the horse and cart," said Stephen. "We can then find ourselves a warm fire and bed down for the night."

Twenty-Two

Tu ne cede malis, sed contra audentior ito

Stephen had little trouble finding the gaol where Lars had been delivered. Every window on the premises had bars; even the door was secured with heavy hinges, double latch on the inside and made from thick, strong wood. The gaol was opposite the town square where it was customary to conduct the hangings. It was a very suitable spot indeed for the hangman's noose, close to the gaol house, and could allow for a large crowd to easily view the proceedings when a man was to be condemned and hung until he was dead. There was a sign upon a bulletin board and in large letters advised, those that could read, that a man was to be committed to the hangman's noose on the morrow. Stephen was quite disturbed by the speed in which Lars had been found guilty, and unless a bribe of some description accompanied the gaoling of Lars, nothing could explain the verdict made in such haste. It was not uncommon to find the most innocent of individuals being hanged for the smallest of crimes, but where power was to be granted, power was to be misused. The rich ruled the roost and the poor were nothing more than pawns to help the rich get richer. To see the filthiest of the poor being swept under a rock and hanged for next-to-nothing was a grand affair for those in power. It was as though they were doing the country a service by ridding it of peasant's blood. Beggars on the streets, in particular around the town's centre, were an eyesore to say the least, let alone the smell of them.

Stephen approached the open door, for at present there was little cause for security measures to be at their highest. The sheriff was seated behind his desk, alone and left to be infuriated by the paperwork that had to be filled, processed, and filed in accordance with the judicial system. He looked up, a seemingly sour man.

"What is it? What can I do for you?"

"My name is Stephen and I am looking for the sheriff of this grand town," said Stephen, giving a little praise to aid him in his future endeavours.

"Aye. Well, you have found him. I am the sheriff." The man of average height put his hand out in greeting. "You can call me Andre."

"Thank you, Andre."

"Are you here to make a report?" asked the sheriff, looking Stephen up and down, seeing a well-stocked man, a youth in simple dress, but not a pauper, beggar or thief. No, this man before him was well educated, he could guess it. The manner of his speech, the way in which he had delivered himself and gave his opening address.

"No, Andre," said Stephen in reply. "I am here to request a meeting, to lay visit upon one of those that you have in your cells."

"We have six in the cells below ground, none in the cells above. Which one of them do you wish to see, and why?"

"I am an old friend who simply wishes to see my former captain before he meets with the hangman tomorrow."

"Ah, you speak of the man with no tongue," said the sheriff, pondering what Stephen had said. "He is a captain, you say. Captain of what?"

"He was one of the men that I fought with during the siege of Constantinople."

"I see," said the sheriff. "And what happened with the siege, may I ask?" "Constantinople has been taken and now lies in Muslim hands."

The sheriff took several paces over to his desk and sat upon it. "My god. You know what this means, Stephen? Europe is next, we are to be consumed."

"Please," said Stephen, interrupting the sheriff of his wayward thinking. "If I could see the man named Lars, then I would be most grateful."

"Indeed. Well, I see why not. He is to be hanged on the morrow, as you have so delicately reminded, but I fail to see what the meeting will bring. He does not talk, you know that."

"I know, but would be grateful for—"

"No more, please, I have much work to do," said the sheriff in a huff. "I shall get the gaoler for you, just wait here."

The sheriff moved over to the door at the rear of the office and pulled a key from his belt, unlocking the door and providing warning. "It is the sheriff; I have a man who wishes to see the prisoner in cell number four." The door opened and the gaoler stood, wine dribbling from his chin, for he was refreshing himself as he normally did. "Take him down and allow him a single lantern. Give him a few minutes." The sheriff turned to Stephen. "The gaoler will give you a lantern and two minutes alone with the prisoner. Do not waste the time you have for I shall not grant a further visit to you or any other of his friends – that is if he has any."

The cell door was opened with much creaking and Stephen entered the cell with the lantern in his hand. The smell from within hit him immediately; the smell of rotting food, of urine and sweat, the smell of the squalor, the filth and the misery, all that he had expected of a dungeon concealed underground with no adequate ventilation or window to speak of.

"Lars, it is I, Stephen."

Stephen swung the lantern around a little until the light fell upon his friend, his clothing like a heap of rags bandaged around him, his eyes peeking through a small opening. Lars was cold, so very cold. Lars was looking forward to the hangman's noose, for the misery of the cell and confinement was too much for his weary bones and old age.

Stephen dashed over and placed the lantern carefully down as the cell door closed behind him, the gaoler letting go with a smirk and a chuckle, showing his true colours: that he cared not for anyone within this dark and infested dungeon.

Stephen and Lars were now alone.

"What have they done to you Lars? Those animals have beaten you." The bruises upon his face could be seen as the lantern flickered, the light spilling across the walls. The eyes in Lars' sockets were his voice that moment, telling of his relief that he could see and hear a friend, the happiness he felt that someone had found him, to hear words of friendship being spoken to him one final time. "If it was not for the burden that I carry... no, it is no burden, but without it I would kill the gaoler and the sheriff for finding you this way." Stephen sat beside Lars and gave him a brief hug before releasing him. "I have news, Lars, and time is short. The secret of the chest is ours, we know of its power and its message. It is so beautiful but also full of devastation. We are going to sea but once again, Lars, to travel to the west, to find a new world which has yet to be discovered by the horrors and misgivings of our civilisation as we know it. From there we are to prepare for the delivery of the Lord's words, but how we are to go about it I do not yet fully know. But you, my friend, will have to remain here. You will not be forgotten. We cannot help you, I am sorry. The only way we can save you is to deliver death to those that have seen to your conviction, and even then some of us may also perish. We must do all we can to protect the orphans."

Lars reached out and grabbed Stephen's arm and smiled a warming smile. Lars understood the predicament as it was and did not feel badly against Stephen's inaction. No one here was at fault except the instigator of his imprisonment, and that man would one day meet his dying day.

"I have spoken to God, Lars, spoken to Him, confronted him man to man, it was a meeting as plain as you see the shadow of my nose cast upon my face on a bright, summer's day. You will not be forgotten when delivered to the hangman, Lars. You will not suffer but will be granted salvation through delivery of a painless death. You will walk in heaven, Lars, that I have been promised. Carry yourself proud for all you have done, show the crowd that you are innocent and not afraid to die, for you have nothing to fear."

Stephen put his hand into his pockets and pulled out the fruit and vegetable that he had placed there earlier when on the cart belonging to Father Ambaedian.

"Something for you, Lars. Hide it well and eat it wisely, for if the gaoler is to see you with it... well, the consequences would be horrendous."

Lars was overwhelmed by the gift of food and placed it immediately out of sight, under his garments. He would eat it all later, a little for his dinner, some for supper, and even a morsel for his breakfast, before his life was surrendered for the pleasure of a few.

"I am sorry I cannot do more," continued Stephen as Lars squeezed his arm before releasing it, showing his understanding, his comradeship, his love for his friend. "But you must believe me; you will not feel any pain when hanged."

Stephen could see by the look in Lars' eyes that he believed every word, that he was not afraid to die, that he was happy to hear of his being delivered into heaven by the grace of God.

A jingling of keys could then be heard as the cell door was opened, the gaoler outside. "I must go now, my friend. Our thoughts will be with you. But you must remember this, too; that God will be with you on your journey into heaven, he will be with you at the time of your death, you have nothing to fear." Stephen took hold of the cross around his neck and spoke his final words of faith. "Give him strength and warmth, take the bitter cold that he feels from his bones, give him special favour in this his last hours on earth." He quickly held the cross out to Lars. "This is the wonder of the chest, Lars, hold it whilst you have the chance, feel it in your fingers."

Lars touched the cross around Stephen's neck and could feel the warmth of his blessed love. Lars then released the cross.

Stephen stood up and grabbed the lantern, departing with one final look, glaring down upon his friend on the cell floor, Lars smiling up at him, and Stephen knew at that moment that Lars had been saved, that he would fend well when it came to dying, that his death would be one of peace, nothing to despair. Lars was warm and happy; he had nothing to be scared about, felt no guilt, and had led a most worthy life.

Twenty-Three

Tu ne cede malis, sed contra audentior ito

Abu and Ahmad had spent their time well since being ashore. With their clothes dry, and being well groomed, they mingled well with the populace of the town known as Barcelona. They had enough money in their pockets to acquire enough food to fill them both, with some left over for a drink at a tavern. They had seated themselves down and were minding their own business when a drunkard raised his voice just a little too much.

"Gold I tell you, a large chest of gold," said the drunkard.

"Where?" asked the other.

"The harbour master of Barcelona; the keeper of the pier. He has much gold in his office, taken from bribes. He has much gold, so much that the chest he conceals it all in is filled to the brim."

"Dirty money," said the other.

"Aye; filthy it is. The man is a criminal if ever I saw one." The drunkard trailed off for a second before continuing. "He is at an official post and uses it to his great advantage. Nothing can be done. All manner of merchandise brought into the harbour gets taxed, but this man... he places his own tax on top of that. And if somebody does not pay... well; they do not get to off-load their goods. Food is spoilt and fresh fish goes bad. What choice do people have? Too hard to make a decent living, too hard it is."

"Aye. It is a shame."

Abu pulled lightly on Ahmad's sleeve and gave him a nod, for Ahmad to follow him outside for some fresh air and private conversation.

"Did you hear all of that, Ahmad?" asked Abu.

"I did, I did indeed."

"There is a chest of gold just waiting for us to pick it up. It seems to me that we should lay visit upon this harbour master, in the dead of night; even possibly the early hours of the morning. Such wealth will serve us well during our stay. What do you say to it?"

"I say we take the chest, as you suggest. The money will go well towards our task. With the wealth of the chest we seek, along with the wealth of the chest on the harbour, we will be very rich, rich beyond our wildest dreams."

"Aye," said Abu. "I thought we would be wealthy when we were one hundred men, but now we are only a handful, the wealth will be unimaginable. The distribution between just a few will be so much more rewarding."

"I can imagine quite a lot, Abu, gold enough to spill from the cup formed by my two hands placed together."

"Yes, me too. Come, let us go and find this chest, take some time to look at the office in which it is kept. I am sure as sure can be that the point of a blade will make the harbour master yelp like he has never yelped before."

Father Ambaedian led the four knights along one of the many piers. There was a carrack, not too dissimilar to the one that Stephen and the others had arrived in, just sitting there, seemingly empty and void of any crew and captain.

"I know the owner of this one," said Ambaedian. "He fishes six mornings every week, brings in his catch and disperses the crew. The goods he sells to merchants, and never have I seen, or heard, of a day that he does not sell. Tomorrow is Sunday and he will not fish. Many of the men will not work on the Sabbath."

"Will it be safe, father, to take this vessel with as much ease as we will require?" asked Raoul.

"The harbour master may interfere. It would be best to have him distracted, but there are many boats, and he cannot watch them all. All he cares for is the wealth that the boats bring in. No, I do not think it will be a problem."

"What about supplies?" asked Martin.

"You will take the sacks of fruit and vegetables that I have in the cart, I insist upon it. The sailors I tend to will not grow hungry or thirsty, for I have plenty of money kept aside. I shall shop for goods tomorrow, after you have departed for the west. I shall bring the cart in along the harbour just minutes before you depart."

"If that does not grasp the attention of the harbour master then I do not know what will," added Raoul.

"Yes, well there is not much we can do about it except hope for the best," said Father Ambaedian. "Besides, what is one man going to do against five?"

"Six," added Lambert, "you forget Stephen."

"Aye. Let us adjourn to the horse and cart, we will wait for Stephen and once he is with us we shall fall upon the hospitality of my friends, for a sleep in front of a warm fireplace." And the meeting with Stephen took place within the half hour. They decided on the action they should take. Martin and Raoul were to aid the orphans in their escape and once successful were to meet Father Ambaedian, Lambert and Bernard, at the horse and cart. Stephen would attend the hanging early to give special prayer. Once all were together at the horse and cart they were to meet Stephen in the main square at the centre of town and make their final way towards the carrack, Father Ambaedian hanging back with the cart until the last moment, so as not to draw attention to the escape. Once all understood and agreed with the action to be carried out they adjourned for the night, taking in the hospitality of Father Ambaedian's friends.

The day wore on like any other and soon the night was upon the city of Barcelona. Abu and Ahmad took turns to stand guard during the night, to await the hour of early morning on which they were to turn to their mischievous behaviour, just hours before the sun was due to rise. They walked so as not to gain the attention of anyone that might be out amongst the cool night air, but the only persons they saw were those too drunk to pinch themselves, let alone be concerned about two sober men out on an early morning's stroll. They approached the harbour master's hut, his place of residence, a small enough premise which afforded the comforts associated with a man of forty, seafaring years. He was asleep, snoring contentedly, dreaming of food, drink, and women of the night. He was a man like any other single man would be, shackled to his way of life, devoted to his treasures and reputation, although his reputation was nothing to boast about, for he was nothing more than a drunk most of the time, and when he was sober he was gambling, moaning about his misfortunes, or shovelling food down his throat.

And so Abu and Ahmad approached from within the shadows cast by the light of the moon, gaining ground on the only door into the master's cabin and the fortune in gold which awaited them both.

Abu opened the creaking door slowly and Ahmad entered first, stepping slowly and with little noise. A little creaking came from the floorboards but the harbour master's snoring saw to it that he slept soundly. The light in the cabin was little, windows letting in light from the moon but was insufficient enough to see the possible whereabouts of the chest of gold. Abu drew up alongside Ahmad and spoke to him in a whisper.

"Sit on him, Ahmad, restraining his arms and torso," said Abu. "I shall grasp his mouth and you get your dagger's blade up against his throat. We will drag the information from him, and if he does not squeal then we shall cut his fingers off, one by one until he does. Do you understand?"

"Yes, Abu; I do."

"Good. Let's get to it."

The harbour master was lying upon a pallet, which itself was made on the floor, to the farthest corner. There was not much to the cabin itself, a table at the side of the room, easily pulled out, plenty of chairs for seating all around, and a workbench along one complete side where the windows were open to the world, where books, charts, and logs would be maintained during the course of a normal business day, stalls for three to be seated, if required.

Ahmad walked over the man on his back and straddled him

slowly before suddenly allowing all of his weight to fall upon him, at the same time bringing the blade of his dagger up to the man's throat. Abu placed his open palm tightly over his mouth, fingers pressing heavily against his lips.

"Shhh. Not a word from you, my friend," said Abu, drawing on the fear that would be welling inside the man on his back. "Do not move, or you die, do you understand." The fear in the harbour master was overflowing but he nodded in general acceptance of his predicament. The last thing he wanted was to die.

"Listen to me, listen carefully," advised Abu. "We come for the chest of gold, that is all. Tell us where it is and you shall live. I shall remove my hand from your mouth and if you attempt to bring alarm to any passer-by then we shall cut into your gullet like you were a dead fish. Do you understand?"

Again the man on his back nodded in acceptance, and little choice he had. Abu pulled his palm from the man's mouth. "Where do you keep the chest of gold?"

"I have no gold, you have been misinformed. I do not—"

Abu thrust his open palm once more over the harbour master's mouth and placed all of his weight from his left knee, onto the man's left arm. "Ahmad, put your weight from your left leg onto his right hand and cut away one of his fingers."

The harbour master cried to scream out in protest, panic striking his eyes, his pupils growing large. He lashed out with his feet to no avail and Ahmad pressed his right hand against the floorboards of the cabin and cut his index finger away from his hand. Blood immediately swamped the area, the harbour master almost fainting with the pain and terror, but he soon calmed down enough for the interrogation to continue.

"Tell me where the chest of gold is or you shall hobble out of here with no fingers and no toes. I am accustomed to issuing pain and cutting fingers off hands. You would be wise to tell us what it is we wish to know. Now, are you ready to try again?" asked Abu.

The harbour master saw no way out and wished to suffer no

more. He could see by the seriousness in Abu's eyes that the man was out to get the chest of gold or cut away every single finger and toe that he had. He nodded in defeat and Abu removed his hand from the harbour master's mouth where gasps of air were the need of the moment. The fat man calmed, pain still showing upon his face.

"Under this pallet upon which I sleep," began the harbour master. "Beneath it are a few loose floor boards. Lift them up and you will see the chest."

Abu and Ahmad unceremoniously moved the harbour master from his pallet to the centre of the cabin floor, Ahmad seating himself once more upon the bulk of the man on his back. Abu withdrew a small dagger and tossed the pallet and bedding to one side. He knocked lightly the floorboards with the handle of his drawn weapon and heard the distinct hollowness from beneath them. He smiled and looked over to Ahmad in his commanding position before placing the blade of his dagger into the slots upon the floor and pried open the secret hiding place. Three boards were removed and a chest could be faintly seen. He put the dagger away and lifted out the chest with huff, for it was extremely heavy. It was a simple box, square in shape, and surprisingly enough had no lock to speak of. Abu simply lifted the latch and then the lid, where the gleaming of the gold coins sparkled in his eyes.

"Ahmad, look," said Abu, mesmerised by what he saw. "Gold, a chest full of it." He pressed his fingers into the coins and played with them, lifting them up and letting them fall, perusing the treasure he had found. "We are rich, Ahmad, all of us, and with the chest of secrets we will be the wealthiest of all Islam."

The harbour master heard what Abu was saying. He could not believe his ears in fact. Islam, these scum that had come to rob him were Muslims.

Abu put the chest down and crawled over to where the harbour master lay, and with the smile on his face, and the look in his eye displaying but pleasure and happiness, he betrayed the fat man once and for all. Abu lashed out with the blade of his dagger; the fat man's screams were muffled as his throat was cut wide open.

"Time to go, Abu," said an anxious Ahmad.

"Wait, not yet. There might be something else of great worth in this station. We must conduct a proper search."

"Very well, Abu, but please, let's not wait around too long."

Twenty-Four

Tu ne cede malis, sed contra audentior ito

Martin and Raoul concealed themselves as best they could, not far from the entrance to the convent, having sought themselves a good vantage point from which to easily see who went in and out of the main door of the building. Being a Sunday morning, and considering that the nuns would have tasks to attend to, in particular to the church service which would obviously distract their attention from the girls, Martin and Raoul considered their plan foolproof. Inside the house was a different matter.

The Mother Superior was busy with her own responsibilities but Sister Bardwell had one main task to attend to on a Sunday morning; she was to prepare the orphans for breakfast and then for the church service. It was understandable that any orphan taken in by the nuns of the convent would be surrendered to religious instruction and that attending church on any day of the week, in particular Sunday, would be accepted as nothing out of the ordinary. How was a little girl supposed to grow up to be a god-fearing adult if the proper tools of knowledge were not installed? And what better way to instil them than having it taught directly from a wife of Christ?

The children this morning did breakfast with the other orphans, of which there were eight. It was not a large number but kept the nuns' hands filled as they jostled around looking after the little ones and maintaining their vows as nuns of the convent. The eight other children were a little older than Catherine and the other twelve, but only by a few years, the oldest being fifteen years of age, almost at full blossom and ready to be married to the first respectable man that came along. The fifteen year old was known as Isabella and was usually quiet and not outspoken. She had been placed in charge of the breakfast this morning as Sister Bardwell had other duties to attend to upstairs, before returning to them, to gather the orphans for the church service. The house maids of the premises were in the kitchen, tidying up what remained of the pots and pans, and the clock in the main room of the house could be heard as it chimed at eight, letting all know that it was time to finish up and get ready for the service to come.

"Come Catherine, you and your friends must hurry. The kitchen staff are very prompt with the errands and our breakfast bowls must be taken into the kitchen on time. The Sisters are very punctual and not apt to accept idleness," said Isabella. "You will find out for yourself, soon enough."

Catherine smiled and accepted the chastisement. "Thank you, Isabella, we shall follow in a few minutes, for some of us require more time."

"Well, please hurry. Once you have finished, take your bowls into the kitchen and depart via the other door, straight to your rooms, comb your hair, brush out the wrinkles in your dress, and wipe the muck from your faces. Sister Bardwell and the Mother will not be pleased with me if you do not come up to scratch."

"We shall not let you down, Isabella," assured Catherine. "Just a few more minutes are all we shall need."

"Very well, I shall see you upstairs shortly, ready for the Sisters' morning inspection of face and dress." With that Isabella and the other seven departed to complete their morning routine, leaving Stephen's girls by themselves.

No sooner had the last of them left the dining area then Catherine was up on her feet. "Quickly, put your things down, all of you, it's time to leave."

The girls knew what was required as Catherine had passed the word to each of them individually, ensuring that each and every one of them understood exactly what they were to do and at the first opportunity that they received. All they had with them were the clothes on their back so there was nothing left for any of them to pick up from within their rooms. They had their cunning, their mischievous cheek, and their beautiful demeanour, like any other child, but their greatest gift, of each and every one of them, was their undying will to be with Stephen and his knights of the cross, for Stephen was like their father, a figure of adulthood that they looked up to with honour, and each had a head-strong devotion to do what they knew was right. If their hearts felt the goodness of the relationship between themselves and Stephen then it must be good, and as long as the feeling of warmth, friendship and love, lasted, they would forever be connected and willing to serve one another.

And so they moved in silence, away from the kitchen, out and away from the dining area, and towards the front door, by which, as the door to a convent and place of regular consoling, it had a very simple locking mechanism that was turned easily.

Martin and Raoul were quickly drawn to the door as it opened slowly, seeing Catherine appear momentarily before she opened it wide and stood aside for the other twelve girls to parade past her, she followed the last of the girls through and closed the door quietly behind her.

Raoul waved the children on ensuring that they could see him, Martin looking at the windows of the convent, making sure that no eyes fell upon their getaway. Sure, the children belonged to them but they knew within the heart of hearts that the Mother Superior would not allow the children to be taken away unless a letter could be obtained from the home in which they wanted to surrender the children, and as no home of any description existed they had no choice but to sneak around like thieves in the night.

Raoul continued waving the children on, a symbolic gesture for them to hurry, to cross the road and approach as quickly as possible. A few passers-by looked upon the action as suspicious, seemingly undecided as to what was happening before them: was it lawful or not? More and more people did stare, picked up by Martin as a concern for their welfare as a group. At the first opportunity he would advise the children, and Raoul, to move briskly but remain as inconspicuous as possible.

The children came to Martin and Raoul with smiles, happy to be away from the convent, even though their stay was accompanied by full bellies and kind words, comfort and warmth. But nothing could compare to the friendship that they had with Stephen and the knights. It was all they wanted in the world, to be loved, to be cared for, even if it meant hardship in life, a life without a mother, without toys, without proper schooling and education. Theirs was a journey to womanhood that none had experienced before them. They were once destined to be slaves in Muslim hands forever, to be abused and tormented, raped and hit and scolded. Stephen offered them so much more than the Sisters of the convent; he had so much more to give. They were now free, free from abuse, free from the pressures offered by an unstable society. They were to commence a journey soon, their last into the unknown, but the first into adulthood. Their futures would be fruitful.

"Come children, this way, and please do not run," said Martin. "We have plenty of time now," and as he spoke those words he looked over his shoulder, worried that they might have been seen. "Come, let's go."

"Sheriff!" The nun was anxious as she entered the gaol.

He looked up and saw a nun before him, dressed in her habit, a cross upon a chain swinging around her neck as she entered.

"Yes, Sister, can I help you?"

"Sheriff, thirteen orphans have been removed from the convent, thirteen children of between five and eight years," she displayed her fretted disposition, confused and upset, "taken from our premises without permission. I fear the worse."

"Please, Sister, sit down," said the sheriff. "I'm sure they are safe, but tell me, what happened?" He was concerned for the time as Lars was due for execution within the next half an hour. The last thing the sheriff needed was a commotion to disrupt his planned morning. He had already sent the gaoler to ensure that the gallows was ready for the prisoner, preparing the hangman for his morning kill, to ensure that the crowd remained reasonably peaceful during the build up to the hanging, but even after all of this there was still much that had to be done."

The Sister sat opposite the sheriff. "I am Sister Bardwell, sent by Mother Superior herself. We think that we know who took the children but they cannot be found anywhere."

"Who, who would take them?"

"Two men, named Martin and Raoul. They brought the children to us and requested a safe haven for them, just for a few days, they said they would return, but this... this is not acceptable, to remove the children in this way. We have no way to prove that it was in fact these two men, but nevertheless, the children desire and deserve the comfort and security of a good home, not to be forced upon the street. And that is the question, sheriff, what are these men to do with thirteen orphaned girls?"

"I see your dilemma, Sister, and I—"

A man suddenly burst through the door, half drunk and almost toppling over his own feet as he entered.

"Sheriff, a word with you," the man stuttered.

The sheriff could not believe his misfortune. "Yes."

"A murder, sheriff, there has been a murder."

"What?"

"It's the harbour master, sheriff, his throat has been cut."

The sheriff was standing and wiped his brow as he thought. He could not believe the morning he was having. "Where's the body?"

"At his place of residence: the harbour. I found him next to his bed, upon the floor with blood everywhere."

The sheriff thought for a second. The dead could wait, the body was not going anywhere, and thirteen orphans would not be too hard to spot, in particular during daylight hours, and the hanging was set to take place soon. "What is your name?"

"Alfred," said the man, out of breath.

"Alfred, go back to the harbour and close the doors, secure them as best you can and I shall be there after the hanging." He looked to the Sister that sat aghast as to the conversation that was taking place, having formed a cross with her fingers upon her chest, giving a prayer for the deceased. "Please, Sister," said the sheriff in as kind a way as he could muster. "Go back to the convent and I shall have some deputies brought to alert. I shall have every street scoured until the children have been found; in actual fact I have several men that are due here shortly."

"Thank you, sheriff, that is most appreciated."

Stephen could not believe the size of the crowd before him. It seemed to him that the entire town had come to see his poor friend die, but at the least they had the solace to know that there would be no pain in death. Lambert and Bernard were currently with Father Ambaedian, awaiting the return of the other two knights and their thirteen orphans. If all went to plan then they would be joined as a group once more.

Stephen watched as the hangman and his apprentice went about their work, preparing the hangman's noose and ensuring that the trap door worked to perfection. The hangman placed a sack filled with soil upon the trap door and the noose was pulled taught around the neck of the sack; he stood aside, pulling on the lever which released the trap door. Some people in the crowd seemed to jump at the noise created by the trap door as it was released, as though struck with horror at the means by which a man was about to die, but nevertheless they still came, flooding the square, pushing and shoving, holding conversation with friends, talking about the man that was about to meet his end.

Stephen remained calm and towards the back of the crowd where he had good visuals all around. As he watched and waited he clutched tight to the cross around his neck, praying for Lars, whether needed or not. The sky was clear and birds filled the sky momentarily, a mass of seagulls heading towards the harbour as though drawn to the smell of fish, but there would be no fishing today. He then pondered the sanity of hanging a man on the Sabbath. The people should be celebrating life, taking time out to honour God, not being fixated by the death of someone none of them knew. So this was what civilisation was coming to, cheap, dirty and uncalled for entertainment?

The crowd moved around like waves upon the ocean, swaying this way and then that, and far to Stephen's right and out of sight was Ibrahim and Sherif, looking over the sea of heads.

Ibrahim continued to look over the crowd as it grew, people gathering from all quarters of Barcelona.

"They will not be here," said Sherif. "They will not take the time to watch a hanging when escape is strong within them."

"Aye, I agree," said Ibrahim, and as he turned he noticed someone, someone in the distance. It was Stephen; he had drawn Ibrahim's attention.

"Sherif–" and Ibrahim was cut off abruptly.

"No names, fool. Do you want the whole of the town to know who we are?"

"I am sorry, you are right, but look, look over there," Ibrahim pointed.

"What am I looking at?"

"That man, the tallest man, young in appearance and clutching something around his neck. He looks solemn and as if in prayer. Do you see him?"

"I do," said Sherif, "but what of him?"

"Do you remember when we were in the Dardanelles, fighting for our lives when attacked by that brigantine?" Ibrahim looked at his friend who was glaring at Stephen. "Do you remember?"

"Yes, yes, I do. What of it, I see no one I recall. You are dreaming. That was a long time ago; forget it."

"I tell you, it is him. Let us try and get a closer look, for I'm sure that what I am looking at is our key to the chest of secrets that we all seek. Come, let's go."

Ibrahim stepped with purpose and with a protest, Sherif followed in his footsteps, moving back away from the crowd as it grew and up a lonely street, taking a shortcut through an alley and then back down towards the centre of town. Suddenly, and with the blindest of luck, they fell upon the other group.

"Abu, Ahmad," said Ibrahim. He looked down at the chest that they carried between them both. "And what is that you have?"

"Gold, Ibrahim, a chest full of gold," said Abu. "There is enough gold in this chest here to make us all very rich men, and once we have found the chest of secrets we will be the wealthiest sons' of wenches that the known world has ever known."

"Let me see," said Sherif greedily. "Open it up, quickly."

"Are you a fool," said Abu. "What if someone was to see us? Do you think it is normal to go parading around showing your chest of gold coins to anyone that passes by? Now forget the gold, it's here and that's all you need to know." Abu looked from Ibrahim to Sherif. "What are you doing here?"

"I have found something, Abu," said Ibrahim.

"He is dreaming," protested Sherif.

Abu looked at Sherif as though disgusted by the interruption. "What did you find, Ibrahim?"

"Do you remember the brigantine in the Dardanelles?"

"Yes, I do; do you think me stupid," answered Abu. "I can see it as though right in front of me as we speak. Never will I forget that boat and the misery it brought me."

"Do you recall when we tried to shackle it with a rope, our endeavour to draw it closer?"

"Yes, yes; come on, quickly with your story, Ibrahim, we do not have all day," said Abu anxiously.

"The man that appeared upon the deck and cut the rope, dodging our ball and arrows, I saw him, now, just minutes ago," Ibrahim was near frantic now, excited beyond measure for bringing such good news to Abu's ear. "We have him cornered amongst the crowd. There is to be a hanging and we will be camouflaged by the mass. We have him, Abu; we can follow him to the chest of his."

All three men looked at Abu as he thought things through. "We will go and watch the hanging, but keep each other close. You, Ibrahim, I want you to make your way slowly towards this man that has cheated death so many times and created so much misery for us all. Stand behind him so that we may all get a good look at him. When he departs the hanging we will follow. We will remain dispersed at first and then join together to fight them when the time is right. We must not be seen, Ibrahim. It is most important that we remain as close as possible to this man, but not too close. Do you understand?"

"I do, Abu," nodded Ibrahim, reflecting upon his task.

"Good. Now be off with you, we will follow and watch you from within the crowd, for I would like to get a good look at this man that has cheated death on so many occasions."

Martin and Raoul made good progress after being hidden for some time far from any prying eye, brought on by the fact that a vast majority of the town's people had laid a visit upon the centre of town to see the hanging that was to take place. The thirteen orphans followed Martin with Raoul bringing in the rear, watching his back to ensure he was not being followed. The distance to the meeting place with Father Ambaedian was on the other side of town but the going was easy. Along the cobbled way and down alley, along several streets and past the rear of the commercial centre of town, a few more streets and then they were upon them, the priest sitting upon his cart in wait with Lambert and Bernard in the rear.

The smiles upon the faces of the children spoke for themselves, seeing the other knights upon the cart bringing joy to all. Catherine, too, was happy but quickly noticed that Stephen was not to be seen.

"Lambert, Bernard, where is Stephen?" asked Catherine.

"He is at the town's square, Catherine," answered Lambert. "He has a duty to perform."

"And what of Lars and Aaron, where are they?"

"We have some bad news for you all, children. Aaron has been murdered and Lars is to be hanged."

The children gasped in horror at the news, refusing to admit that Lars could be guilty of anything that would condemn him to death.

"Lars is innocent," said Catherine. "Stephen knows that he could not do any wrong."

136

"We all know this, child," answered Father Ambaedian. "But we must accept fate as it has been dealt us."

"Who are you?" asked Catherine as politely as she could.

Ambaedian looked into the child's eyes and saw not a child but a fully grown adult. He had not asked many questions in regards to the children so knew not of their character or real suffering. Were they intelligent? Did they deserve any particular recognition? What was their disposition?

"I am Father Ambaedian," answered the priest, and trying to bring immediate closure to the unnecessary questioning, added one simple measure of information. "I am Stephen's friend and know everything there is to know about him."

Catherine considered the information for what it was worth. "How did Aaron die?"

"Unnecessarily," answered Lambert. "But let's concentrate on our situation, Catherine. Father Ambaedian has found us a new boat, so that we can leave this place."

"A new carrack?" she asked. "What of the old one?"

"Look, Catherine," interrupted Bernard. "There is much to our situation that you may not understand, but we do not have the time to discuss it all now. Trust in your peers and we will be away from this town as soon as we possibly can. We are going by way of the town's centre to get Stephen and from there we shall go to the carrack that awaits us. You will be escorted around the scene of Lars' death but in close enough contact for security to remain present. You must adhere to all commands that are given to you," Bernard looked around to all the children. "All of you children, do you hear? All of you must remain calm. All of you must heed every word that is asked of you. You must not falter in any way for to do so could see you back in the convent and under the care of the nuns. Now, it is time to go. Stay close children for there could be danger lurking behind every corner."

Stephen looked on as the time finally arrived for Lars to appear on the scene. The hangman and his apprentice were stood fast upon the platform of death where a single rope hung from a cross beam between two posts, a loop large enough to be inserted over a head formed at the end as it dangled freely, waiting for its victim, silently swinging a little, like a pendulum. The crowd suddenly grew silent as heads shifted left and right, each person trying to get a look at the guilty. The cart upon which Lars was being delivered to the hangman's noose finally came into view, and as the single horse-drawn cart moved into the centre of town, the crowd commenced with their interaction with the proceedings. Shouts and laughter erupted from all that watched, pointed fingers and mocking, pieces of rotten fruit being hurled through the air. The frame of the cage in which Lars was secured did little to protect him from what was thrown. He could not dodge or crouch down because he was restrained in an upright position. The sheriff walked beside the horse-drawn cart, a deputy leading the horse calmly up front, whispering gentle words into the horse's ear, keeping the animal from acting abruptly or trying to flee the scene. The horse had done this duty many times in the past but it was hard to get used to the screams of the crowd, even harder to escape the odd piece of fruit as it came tumbling through the air, hitting him in the flank.

The cart came to a stop at the foot of the hangman's gallows and the sheriff clambered aboard where the cage enclosed Lars, untying his secondary bonds and removing him, hands still tied behind his back, to the steps beyond.

Stephen could see that Lars was solemn, at peace with the world. A piece of fruit then hit him in the head to which the sheriff turned abruptly, for it had nearly hit him. They continued up the short climb to the hangman in wait.

The sheriff handed the convicted over and moved to the side allowing those within the square to see clearly from wherever they stood, a hood being prepared for Lars. Death was only minutes away when Lars looked up and saw the drunken sailor, John, the one that was to be his herald when danger was near, and John looked away, ashamed, and then Lars saw Stephen to the rear of the crowd, hand upon his chest, the cross hanging there beneath his fingers. It was his salvation to have seen the cross for himself, when Stephen laid visit upon him in the dungeon of Barcelona. He did not feel alone, he did not even stand alone, for at that moment he felt the presence of the Lord from high above, and then the hangman's hood was unceremoniously placed over his head. The bright of day now passed his vision for ever but the noise of laughter and dread could still be heard. It all flowed through him but did not sting, the horrors of those last few minutes were blotted out by something with more power than he had ever experienced before. And as the sheriff began a brief sentencing to death, Lars could only hear the sweet voice of heaven, for he was being accepted by God like any other good Christian who was pure of heart. He would walk in heaven, passing the golden gates, embraced by the almighty Father who looked, not down upon him, but from beside him.

The noose was then passed over the hood and placed taught against his neck, but Lars only felt the caressing of someone that cared, he could smell the blossom of roses, of perfumes, the essence of nectar. Death was not consuming him, it was being accepted, and as the trap door was released by the hangman, the crowd grew quiet and Lars was uplifted to be with God.

Stephen could see what no other could see. He felt what no other could feel. His friend, the Teutonic, transcended into heaven. And Lars was happy, empty of dread, and now Lars was looking down upon the square, wondering as to why so many people, who did not know who he was, would want to see him die this way.

His eternal life had just begun.

Twenty-Five

Tu ne cede malis, sed contra audentior ito

Ibrahim stood patiently behind Stephen and could see his Muslim comrades off to the side, each looking in his direction, a suspicious group of men indeed.

It was then that Stephen made his move, putting the cross well away inside his shirt and drawing his attention to the task at hand. There was nothing further he could do for Lars, for he was beyond any further help. His life was in God's hands now.

So Stephen stepped off towards the edge of the square, commencing the short trek to the harbour and the carrack that waited. It was then that lady luck struck for just ahead he saw the four knights and thirteen children. Martin was at the rear.

"Martin," shouted Stephen, loud enough for the knight to hear his call, and with his herald came the turning of heads as each of the children stopped in their tracks and rushed the man they loved so dearly like a herd of thirsty cattle to a watering hole.

The joy of the meeting fell from the children's lips, each asking how he was, where he had been, how wonderful it was to see him again. And the thought came like a rush to Stephen that these children did indeed love him with all their heart for he had only been gone a short time, but even a short time for the group of orphans was like an eternity. Never again did they wish to be separated from their father figure, their friend, their knight of knights. Hugs and affectionate pats on the head were exchanged with great exuberance. The smiles upon the children's faces were contagious, and all of the knights forgot, just for the moment, what their task was. Everything seemed to be so unimportant. They were a family unit, one and the same, and to separate the family reunion was beyond contemplation, but it was soon to be revealed that two of the group were to remain behind in Barcelona, for Stephen had picked up on a vision of the future where explorers from right across Europe did take to the waters of the Atlantic to flood the New World with their greed and condemnation of Indian life. The future was filled with so much treachery that the horrors of Stephen's dreams could not have been anticipated.

Ibrahim was again standing at Abu's side, stepping up to the group of three as they watched with great interest the group of knights and children.

"Do you see the chest anywhere?" asked Abu of the others, but no answer came, just shakes of the head and dumbfounded silence. "We shall follow them to wherever it is they lead us. They will have to attend the chest soon and wherever it is, there are sure to be other men guarding it. We are outnumbered and must sway the disadvantage to our favour. We must approach unseen and ambush in a manner that ambush is not known. We must strike with a surprise attack but not until we are sure of where to find the prize." Abu looked briefly at the others. "Do you all understand?" and Abu looked no further than the expressions upon their faces, the twinkle in their eyes, their silence demeanour. "I see you do. We must move as a group but remain apart. If we are too close together we will be advertising our presence too freely. Let us go now and seek our fortune."

The group of knights and thirteen orphans recommenced their walk towards the harbour where the carrack awaited them. Abu and the other three men of Islam followed in wide stride, maintaining a good distance from the Christian group.

The sheriff moved in alongside the deputy, who had returned to the seat upon the cart. "Morgan," said the sheriff, drawing the deputy's attention. "Take the body to the morgue as soon as you can and then head back to the gaol. I shall be a little while. I have a task to attend to at the harbour."

"What is it, sheriff?"

"It seems that the harbour master was killed in his sleep last night, or first thing this morning. I do not think there is much we can do. Oh, and Morgan; keep your eye open for thirteen children wandering around in a group. There will be two men with them."

"I shall. What should I do if I see them?"

"Follow them if you can, find out where they are or where they are going... let me know as soon as possible so that we can return them to the convent. Be wary of the men travelling with them, please be warned, and take as much precaution as required, I cannot emphasize that enough."

"I shall do just that, sheriff."

The sheriff nodded as the orders were accepted and stepped back and then around, to move from the square, through the crowd as it dispersed, and towards his next duty.

It did not take long for him to push his way through the throngs for most individuals, knowing of his status, stepped back to allow him through; it was then, as he reached the furthest edge of the town's centre, that up front and in the distance he could see the group of thirteen children and several men moving along with them. It was quite clear from what he saw that the children were not distressed as some of them were skipping along the cobbled way and others held the hands of some of the adults, looking up into their eyes with a smile. And as he pondered the situation, with his continued walk towards the pier, he saw four other men moving, two to each side of the street, moving as though to maintain their distance from the group to their front. The sheriff stopped momentarily and considered the situation. Were the four men following doing so as a rear guard action to the first group? Were they following for reasons of abduction? Had the Mother Superior organised for some vagabonds to search for the children, funded by her own purse? It all seemed very strange to him, but if one thing was for sure, the group of four men were most definitely following the group to their front. It was then that he saw the chest carried between two of them. Money perhaps, to offer for the purchase of children.

Slave traders; that was the answer. He would have to move carefully, watch from a distance, and when the time was right he would move in with help gained from any source to rescue the poor children.

Stephen ushered the children on, becoming concerned for those that followed. He had picked up on the movement of the undesirables through sheer luck, when he looked out towards the rear to consider what he was to say to Martin and Raoul.

"Come children. Stay up with Lambert and Bernard, do not dawdle, for time is short." They continued on past him as he drew in alongside both Martin and Raoul, taking up stride between them both.

"Martin, Raoul, there is something I must say to you both, and listen to me carefully you must." He looked them both briefly in the eye and could see their mystifying glances, as thou the weight of the world was upon them. They could both tell by the tone of Stephen's voice that something was coming their way, something that was not going to be altogether pleasing, but completely necessary. They had been together for so long that they sensed when one had bad news to tell the other, checking the tone of one when they spoke, understanding the body language as though it spoke with its own voice.

"Do not be alarmed and please do not look behind you. We are being followed by four men. I do not know who they are but I am guessing by their dress that they are sailors, possibly those from the brigantine that was following us. But listen to me, regardless of who they are and what they are doing I have a task that must be performed, something for you both that will not be to your liking. Listen and listen carefully for I can say this only once. We are close to the harbour and the pier of our interest, and are short on time. The voices and dreams... pictures if you like, pictures I see within my head, they are sometimes very hard to decipher and come at the strangest times. But I see a man and a woman, a pair of vicious heathens who are tempted to take what they can, a man and a wife that are as impure as the devil himself. They seek to bring harm to us, but I do not know how.

They are close, I can feel them, but do not know where they are. But nevertheless, regardless of this, you two good men must serve me as though you would serve the Lord Himself. I am going to ask something of you both and it will not be to your liking. You must come with us to the harbour but once we are there you must remain in town. You must stay in town for several weeks at least, to ensure that we are not followed. It is the man and the women who I fear the most." The two knights said nothing as they continued walking. "The Lord has provided you with special permission to use any force necessary to prevent the New World from being discovered. It will be inevitable, one day, but time must be had for us to prepare the defences for the Cross of Christ. Time is of the essence." Stephen looked up and saw the pier stretching out upon the harbour to his front. "We are nearly there. I am sorry, Martin, Raoul. There is nothing for it. You must do the Lord's will and remain alert, remain in Barcelona and cover our tracks, do all you can to prevent others from following in our wake."

Twenty-Six

Tu ne cede malis, sed contra audentior ito

Before reaching the pier, Martin and Raoul were sent upon their quest. "This is it," said Stephen. "Do not come any closer; the departure will be too much for the children to bear. We cannot afford a lengthy goodbye for it will delay us more than we can afford."

"We understand," said Martin. He put out his hand in farewell to Stephen who returned the gesture, slapping him on the shoulder as he did so; Raoul did the same.

"It has been an honour serving with you," said Raoul. "I would not have wished my departure from Káros to have been by any other means. I served the Lord on that island of solitude and will continue to serve here in Barcelona. We, both of us, will continue to serve as we have always done."

"I am happy to hear such words," said Stephen, "and am humbled too, by your courage and service. But one last thing, good men. If a fight is to be drawn here upon this pier, with those that are following, you must not attempt to aid us. You both must live in order to carry out your task, it is most important."

They smiled and let each other go, Martin and Raoul turning on their heels and departing in a hurry, for they did not wish to upset the children who had nearly reached the pier. They moved with such haste that they skirted behind a building and out of view before any of the children could grow wise to what was happening, and Stephen turned and raced off to catch up with the others.

It was at this time that the first of the children turned around to look behind. She could see that Stephen was by himself, that

Martin and Raoul had disappeared. A few of the others now did the same, looking behind in wonder as to what was going on.

Stephen reached them and looked down upon them. "Martin and Raoul have been commanded by God to attend an important mission. We will continue without them. They will, forever, remain in our memories. Come, children, we have no time to waste, we must be going now." They continued on their way without further ado, only a little distance remaining between them and the carrack. It was then that the Muslims caught sight of the group at the harbour that they were heading for and Abu brought a temporary close to the follow-up.

Abu could see the carrack, which was of obvious interest to Stephen and the others, for they were heading directly towards it. Abu called the others over to the side, behind a small dwelling situated opposite where the pier began, two of the men seen moving away from the others, sleeking off quietly before quickening their stride, away from the others.

"The carrack at the end of the pier must be the one," said Abu to the other three. "That is the one." They huddled together in order for Abu to let his strategy be known. "When a majority of them have gone aboard we will rush them. We have no other option, for the children will only get in our way... at least the fight now looks to be in our favour."

"No, let us wander up as close as we can get," said Ibrahim. "Let us close the gap a little, at least. It will give them less time to prepare themselves for the fight to come."

"Very well," agreed Abu. "We shall wait. Let us watch now."

They watched as the children were helped aboard the carrack and Alfred, the drunken sailor who had reported to the sheriff earlier on in the day, exited the cabin where the body of the harbour master lay cold.

"Who are you?" yelled Alfred. "What are you doing? That boat belongs to—" and without much effort the sailor was silenced, for Stephen had quickly placed his hand upon the hilt of his sword and withdrew it slightly. Abu saw this action and deemed it as a defence, not realising that a man had appeared at the doorway to the cabin of the harbour master, for the door was not facing them.

"Now, quickly, let's go," shouted Abu and the group of four were running up the pier, Ibrahim and Sherif still porting the chest of gold. "Let us take them down."

"Lambert, Bernard, a call to action if you do not mind," said Stephen, bringing the situation to the attention of the two knights as calmly as he could. They were upon the planks so sturdy via quick responsive action, standing in front of the boat and with swords drawn, and all before the Muslims were upon them, the chest of gold being dropped in earnest, and the fight was underway. The metal scraping of sword against sword brought terror to the ears of Alfred, who by now had sealed himself in the hut. The children, being used to the fighting between men, having been exposed to the horrors blood and death, simply took cover where cover could be sought along the pier-side of the carrack, and watched as the fighting commenced.

Catherine looked to the other children, quite unaware that what they were on was a simple civilian boat, but brought immediate attention to them all. "Quickly, sisters, we must find weapons, spears, anything to aid Stephen and the others." The children dispersed as quickly as they had initially sought cover and started their search for anything that would help the fight to fall in their favour, and it was not long before Lois jumped from the carrack to pier, and with a harpoon in her hand.

Lois could see through her eyes so wide that one of the Muslim's had already been killed, for he lay upon the deck with blood pooling out of his chest, Sherif, motionless and with eyes wide open, looking up into the sky. Bernard had his sword temporarily stuck in his gut and was trying to pull it free, which he did after a brief struggle. She shook this from her senses, and seeing her opportunity, speared Ahmad in the gut, just missing Lambert's thigh as she thrust her weapon forward. The big man immediately let his sword fall to the pier as he clutched at his wound, blood appearing at his mouth. He pulled away from the spear and stumbled to the side, falling from the pier and into the water of the harbour, putting the fight in favour of Stephen and the two knights. Bernard then swung around to look for another to fight as did Lambert when the incomprehensible occurred.

Catherine had appeared upon the pier and before she could aid in the fight she was grabbed from behind, the blade of a dagger expertly held against her neck. It was Abu, he had seen his opportunity, and feeling within every vein of his body that the men cared for the children, enough to give their lives to protect them, took this as his only means to secure victory.

"Not a move! Cease your action!" Abu's voice penetrated all, everyone's attention gained in less time that it takes to blink. Stephen stood firm, and had ceased to fight with Ibrahim. Lambert and Barnard were also drawn from their closure, the fight against their opponents having been victorious.

Ibrahim pivoted from side to side, covering the three men as best he could. At any moment both Ibrahim and Abu could be dead men. The fight being initially in their favour was soon turned around, but now, with Catherine's throat resting upon Abu's blade, the fight looked to be in Muslim hands.

"You, the tall one," said Abu. "What is your name?"

"Stephen."

"Then, Stephen, listen to me. All we want is the chest; the chest of secrets. Give it to me and the girl shall live."

"We do not have it," replied Stephen. "It was lost at sea."

"You lie," added Abu. "I should warn you that I can grow impatient and very quickly." A look of seriousness fell upon his face. "Where is the chest?"

"We do not have it, it was lost."

"If you do not tell me where it is then I shall run my blade across this girl's throat. I am not afraid to kill the innocent."

Stephen looked at Abu and saw in him a cowardice hidden beneath the masquerade. "If you kill her then we will be upon you like a pack of hungry wolves."

"Ibrahim," Abu looked to his left. "Take their weapons."

Ibrahim shifted slightly but was brought to an immediate stop.

"One move, Ibrahim," said Stephen, "and you will die, followed shortly by the death of your master, who I shall take much pleasure in torturing to death."

"Oh, how shrewd you are," said Abu. Silence dominated the scene whilst everyone on the pier assessed the situation. "What do you suggest, Stephen?"

"Let the girl go and you shall live," said Stephen in reply.

"No; no, no, no, no. That simply will not do. I tell you what I shall do. I shall take this little one with me and when I am clear of the harbour I shall let her go."

"Let her go?" asked Stephen with a note of sarcasm.

"Certainly. Why? Do you not trust me?" asked Abu, a question which could only be answered in one way, and that was by way of a quarrel, for from the deck of the carrack a shot had been released from a crossbow, a weapon which one of the sailors of the boat employed against sharks when at sea. All of the girls had been taught to use the weapon at one time or another, taught by their friend, Lars. It was in memory of the man with no tongue that the shot released was so well delivered that Abu would have had no idea, whatsoever, what had been delivered to him. The quarrel entered through his right ear and penetrated out through his left, a shot so skilfully fired that it was beyond belief. Abu simply fell to the pier like a sack of potatoes. Without further ado, Lambert, Bernard and Stephen, encircled the lone Ibrahim.

"The offer of survival has expired. You can either die fighting or die a coward. How will you be delivered to your unholy God?" asked Stephen with as less pity than Ibrahim would feel kicking out at a cat.

Ibrahim looked at the three as they surrounded him and a grimace grew upon his mouth, a snarl being formed. He lifted his sword and charged at Stephen, for he was to blame for all he had suffered. Within seconds, Ibrahim lay in a pool of his own blood and a rattling noise from the boards of the pier struck Stephen's ears. He lifted his head and saw that Father Ambaedian was making his way towards them, sacks of fruit and vegetable nested in the cart, ready to be transferred to the boat.

"Lambert, throw that filth into the sea. Bernard, get ready your hands for some heavy lifting," commanded Stephen and turning to the girls continued with his delegations. "Girls, all of you, forget what you have seen here today and know that you have done well. Lars would be proud to have seen you fight today. When the supplies have been placed upon the boat's deck I wish you to drag them; pile them, along the centre of the boat as best as possible; we'll store them later. Our voyage commences immediately."

Stephen had time to turn his attention to the harbour and pier when the priest pulled up in his horse drawn cart.

"Father Ambaedian, just in time," greeted Stephen. "If you climb down to the pier, be careful, there is plenty of blood here to send even the sure footed onto his backside."

"I thank you for your warning, Stephen. I shall pray for the devils a little later but for now we must get the supplies to the boat," and the priest turned to the movement of the cart as Lambert climbed aboard to throw the sacks down to Bernard and Stephen. "Ah, already in place. Good to see good men, doing a good day's work."

The sacks were quickly taken from cart to the boat where the children, being thankful for being provided the opportunity to assist, and Stephen, thankful for the opportunity to take their minds away from the slaughter they had just witnessed, placed them along the centre line of the carrack.

Within just a few minutes the cart was empty. "Thank you, father, for all you have done," said Stephen, shaking the priest's hand.

"It has been a pleasure to see the birth of something so grand. I just hope that with the time you have to contemplate life that a solution can be found by which can be delivered unto the world."

"I do too, father. The cross has a purpose, and whether we call it the Holy Grail or the Cross of Christ, matters little, for we both know what it is. A solution has to be found. I am confident that one day I too shall walk in heaven, but that day is a long way off. These thirteen children I have with me will be long deceased themselves before I can even consider my time on earth as expired. But even with so much time, none of it shall be wasted."

"I believe you, my son," said Ambaedian, looking down upon Stephen as he picked up the reins once more. "Oh, I nearly forgot." He moved over to the side of the cart and lifted out the basin. "Here, take this."

"Thank you, father."

"I shall be off now and wish you a quick and healthy voyage. I'm sure God will see to it that you will be provided supplies along the way, whether such supplies be provided by the sea, a coastal town, or passing galleon. A journey like yours does not go unrewarded."

"Thankyou for your kind wishes and I bid you a good day. Good luck to you."

"And to you; all of you."

The priest waved to the children as they stood upon the deck of the boat and Martin and Raoul prepared the carrack for sailing. The work to get her underway was going to be hard, for there was much to be done and only three adults to do all of the work, but as Father Ambaedian had noted, a journey like theirs did not go unrewarded.

Stephen turned to approach the carrack and as he turned he almost fell over the chest of gold. He looked down upon it and knew instantly what it carried. There was no temptation to open the chest, no urge to take it for himself or the others. The carrack they were taking did not belong to them and had not been paid for. The message in his head was simple. Leave the chest and the end of the pier for the owner of the carrack would find it soon enough.

Stephen jumped aboard the carrack and the sails were unfurled, a wind coming up from behind them. As they commenced their great journey the owner of the carrack miraculously appeared, running towards them, shaking a fist, and as he closed the gap he slipped upon some blood and fell upon the chest. Mystified, he opened it. He cupped the gold up in his hands and looked up to see Stephen waving a hearty farewell. They did not know each other, had never met, but at that moment the owner of the carrack felt that justice had been served him and that the price paid was in his favour. He waved back with a smile that quickly turned into a look of disbelief and he picked up the chest of gold, taking it with him as he departed: but struggling heavily with its weight.

Twenty-Seven

Tu ne cede malis, sed contra audentior ito

Martin came to a stop.

"Wait, Raoul," Martin felt the sudden surge to assist Stephen and the others. "We must go back and fight."

"No," replied Raoul. "We must do as we have been requested."

"Even if it is wrong to sit back and do nothing?"

"Nothing is exactly what we need to do. Look. Over there, Father Ambaedian is heading towards the pier. Do you see?"

"Aye. Let us wait a little. I feel something within me?"

"What is it?"

"I do not know," said Martin, searching himself for an answer. He looked up again and saw two figures within the shadows of the houses upon a street corner. "Look over there. What do you see?"

"Why, it's a man and a woman," answered Raoul.

"A man and his wife," corrected Martin. "Let's watch them and see what they do."

"Do you think they are the ones that Stephen had warned us against?"

"Who else would be sneaking around, following the priest like a cat would follow a mouse?"

So the two men watched in anxious wait to see what would eventuate, and minutes later Martin pointed off to a point alongside the pier. "Look yonder." A man was running towards the pier, his fist shaking, punching the air. "Who is that?"

"I have no idea, but let's concentrate on the couple."

The two knights slunk back into the shadows themselves and

watched from their safe station, some distance from where commotion was about to be brewed.

Father Ambaedian let the horse pull the cart slowly from the harbour where the goodbyes had been exchanged. He was happy and fulfilled, a smile upon his face letting the world know that he could not be more content with his life than he was this minute in time. His smile was so well cast that Martin and Raoul could see his jubilance from where they stood.

Quite suddenly, and without warning, the sheriff of the town jumped out to confront the priest, taking hold of the horse's bridle to prevent it from galloping away, even though such action was the furthest thing from Ambaedian's mind.

"Good morning, sheriff," said Father Ambaedian. "How is your day?"

The sheriff peered up into his eyes and took the bridal into his left hand, releasing his hold with the right and preparing himself for what might come, his hand hovering over his sword on his left side. The priest was amused. "I saw you, father. I saw it all. The fight upon the pier; aiding the escape of the orphans. I want answers from you, father, I want answers and I want them now." The fat on the man jiggled slightly as he sang in his threatening tune. It seemed to the priest that the sheriff thought him guilty, or in the least, directly responsible for the killings upon the pier. "You tell me what I want to know or I'll have you upon the gallows before you can give praise to the Lord."

"Sheriff, I have no idea what you are talking about," replied Ambaedian. They locked eyes and the sheriff's heart missed a beat, a sudden pain was felt scrambling down his left arm, and then the crushing pain upon his chest made him gasp for air. He collapsed.

"Sheriff, sheriff, are you all right?" Ambaedian was now worried for him, regardless of the threats, and he knelt down beside the fallen man. He felt for a pulse and realised immediately that he was dead. The sheriff's heart had given to the stresses of an unhealthy lifestyle, where drinking ale and wine had finally dealt its final blow. Being a man of faith and without further ado, Father Ambaedian lifted the sheriff, with great effort, onto the cart. He would deliver him to the closest church; it was the least he could do.

Martin and Raoul watched the couple from where they stood.

Henry looked into his wife's eyes, open palms holding onto shoulders. "Did you see all of that, Patricia?" he asked of his wife.

"I did. I saw it all," she said in reply. "What shall we do now? The boat has sailed, a voyage into the west. We have no hope of laying our fingers upon the gift of God."

"No. No, we do not," said Henry, thinking as best he could on the scenario before him. "We must deliver the news to the sailors of the tavern, the one between here and the town's centre; you know the one."

"I think it's called the Sea Witch."

"Yes, that's it. I know from past experience and much conversation that only the bravest of sailors drink there. Men from right across Spain and France, Portugal and Italy. We must tell our story, Patricia, tell it to the world. We only need one person to believe us."

"But what good will it do? It will not make us rich."

"Maybe not, Patricia," and Henry released his hold on his wife. "But the Holy Grail. It cannot be wasted upon a land where its very goodness will be lost forever."

"Do you really believe that there is land in the west?"

"We have to, my wife. We must believe it in order to convince someone, anyone, that great salvation is to be had. It could be worth much gold to us. Imagine if the Holy Grail was found... what percentage of its worth do you think we would be paid?"

"None, husband, for the greed of those I know, that sail upon the sea, would turn their back on you and run for the hills. Believe me, there is no wealth to be had now."

"Maybe you believe that, but I do not. I must try to do what I believe is right, regardless of your solid opinion."

"I understand, Henry. You must do what you must do."

"Thankyou, Patricia. I love to hear your words of encouragement."

"So what will you do now?"

"I shall go to the tavern. You can go back to the cart and then home."

"When can I expect you back at the house?"

"Before nightfall," said Henry, taking his wife in his hands and kissing her solidly. "For I love nothing more than sharing a bed with you."

And across the other side of the road, Martin and Raoul saw the man and the woman exchange much in conversation, and then the kiss came and the wife walked off in the direction of her home. The smithy could be seen to look left and right before he stepped onto the cobbles and started for the Sea Witch.

"There he goes," said Martin of the obvious. "We must follow him, see where he goes. I feel it in my bones, as I thirst for water and hunger for food."

"Very well," agreed Raoul, "we shall see what he does."

The carrack was well out to sea and all aboard her had made themselves familiar, and comfortable, with their surrounds. It was in much likeness to their previous boat. The sacks of fruit and vegetable were carried below deck at the first opportunity and once everything that had to be completed was finished, Stephen called out to Lambert, Bernard, and the thirteen children.

"It is time to deliver the basin and its contents into the sea," said Stephen. "Never again will it see the light of day."

All watched as Stephen picked up the basin from where it sat next to the main mast and moved over to the port side of the carrack.

"There is no ceremony for the burial of something so sacred," said Stephen, "so I shall forego giving any sermon. Instead I shall simply do this." And he dropped the basin overboard. It quickly filled with water and commenced to sink, disappearing from the surface of the sea, to fall to its final resting place beneath the waves of the Mediterranean. Stephen looked to the two knights. "Some would think that this is the end, that the delivery of the basin into the mouth of the sea was the conclusion of our adventure. But I tell you this; our journey has only just begun."

Henry was standing in front of thirty seated sailors, all of whom wore swords upon their waists. Tankards filled the tabletops and the thick conversation was quickly brought to a close.

"Hear me, hear me all, for I have something of great importance to tell you," yelled Henry, and having gained the attention of the sailors, quickly continued. "I will be quick with you but if you wish to hear more then I can comply, for the information I am about to disclose will make some of you very rich men."

Some of the sailors that had tankards in their fists put them down, they were all ears. The smithy was singing their tune, the tune of wealth.

"I have seen with my own eyes something of great worth and it is escaping, drawing further away from us as we speak, aboard a carrack which is sailing for the west, it must be— " Suddenly the spirited speech was brought to a close for the slamming of the inn's door made Henry turn with a jolt. Before him were two men, two men who were standing side by side.

The silence within the tavern that minute was profound, not a single noise heard. And then the silence was broken by the two knights, Martin and Raoul, for they both drew their swords from their sheaths and stepped towards their destiny; the protection of the Cross of Christ.

Epilogue

Tu ne cede malis, sed contra audentior ito

History is plagued with reports of the Holy Grail, of its existence and where it can be found. One story above all others tells of its existence in France, on the coast of the Mediterranean, at a place called Renne le Chateau. It is also fair to say that tales of El Dorado and the Amazons have flooded the minds of Conquistadors, as it did the Incas that preceded them. How true were such stories and how much emphasis should be permitted to ride on the hearsay and word-by-mouth tales? Tales too flourished of natives whose feet were literally affixed their legs back-to-front, whereby they would appear to have been walking one way, where in fact they were travelling the other; so much for the instinct of the tracker. A creature which was half man and half llama was also present upon the wind of tale. It should be considered, and needless to say, that the communication barrier did also loan itself to the calamity of confusion when trying to decipher and understand a foreign tongue. Where did the stories come from? From trade? Trade with the Indians of the Amazon forest was rudiment to comfort, though the wealth of trade was something not sought by many of the Indians of the forest, in particular those along the coast, at the mouth of the Amazon, the door to a New World of people and animals alike.

Stories rose upon the tongue of the Spanish invader of a man covered in gold, the Golden Prince. It was said, via various sources, that he bathed in the lake of clear blue water, which, when emerged, he found himself coated in the dust of gold. On occasion, where ceremony was sought, he was said to anoint his body with a specific substance prior to entering the waters to bathe. But it was not just the gold that triggered an inner greed to grow, but also the promise of wealth secured through trade; the trade of cinnamon. And did the Golden Prince actually, as reported, send tribute to female warriors that housed themselves in buildings of stone, where feathers of parrots were employed to cover the roofs of their dwellings, a symbol of divinity when placed upon the supports of a roof on a temple.

Stones of green were also spoken of, a symbol of native belief in the supernatural world of mysticism, a representation of the green of the forest; and preach they did, in a way unclear to the Spanish, preaching conducted whilst facing the East, the direction know and believed to house the spirit whom had so long ago visited the Amazon's world of mystery and beauty. Was the East in fact their homeland?

El Dorado is translated as The Gilded Man, which means to cover with gold, make golden, or paint gold. The Golden One; one who is made of gold, due to his stature as ruler, decision making, and the way in which he commanded over others: the chosen one.

Stephen was the Golden Prince and the thirteen orphans were the legacy of the Amazon. Their story remains unknown, sealed by the curtain of darkness, shrouded by the jungles of Brazil. Do they still exist; are they still present upon the land of the New World?